Hidden Talent
Forest Glen Suspense, Book Three
Bettie Boswell

www.MtZionRidgePress.com

Mt Zion Ridge Press LLC
295 Gum Springs Rd, NW
Georgetown, TN 37366

https://www.mtzionridgepress.com

ISBN 13: 978-1-968693-10-7

Published in the United States of America
Publication Date: January 1, 2026
Copyright: © 2025 Bettie Boswell

Editor-In-Chief: Michelle Levigne
Executive Editor: Tamera Lynn Kraft

Cover art design by Tamera Lynn Kraft
Cover Art Copyright by Mt Zion Ridge Press LLC © 2025

Chapter One

Carlton Marsh surveyed the crowded hallway. Superheroes and robotic figures intermingled with winged fairies and hunchbacked trolls. He wondered why in the world he'd agreed to the assignment. A comic convention was the last place he ever dreamed of attending.

Babysitting paranoid cartoonist, Mara Shore for a late afternoon autographing session, in a convention center full of delusional adults wasn't what he imagined for his first assignment with Guardians Security Group. His new employer and former federal boss, **Kent Russell**, probably thought the job would be safe enough for a limping ex-fed. Who would have thought that at age thirty he'd trade in his badge for a new career? At least it paid well. His only complaint was that the woman was a mule lover. To top it off, months ago, one wild mule had helped cripple his chances of continuing in his government job.

He leaned heavily on his cane and followed the petite figure in front of him. She struggled to push forward through the mingling mob. A dark Stetson sat low on her brow. A jet-black braid swayed down her back, calling attention to her athletic body. She'd wrapped her tanned arms around a tote held close to her chest. His client would never make it to her destination at this rate.

He tapped her on the shoulder. "Miss Shore, would you like me to lead? I can get us to Hall B quicker by blazing a trail for you to follow."

She frowned and waved him into the lead. He felt her hand lightly touch his back as they forged ahead. Warmth from her small palm shot a sense of protectiveness through him. At least he could do something for the fearful woman. Between his bulk, the pounding cane, and the frown he knew graced his face, the stream of people flowing toward them divided, providing a path for forward movement.

A pinching grab on his shoulder made him pause and turn to his client. "Is everything all right, ma'am?"

She stretched on her tiptoes and leaned closer to his ear. A light whiff of apple scent hung in the air between them. "There's a guy in a pharaoh mask off to our right. He keeps looking this way and heading the same direction as us."

"I'll take note of him, Miss." Carlton wanted to laugh at her fears. Instead, he concentrated on moving toward their destination. A vast number of people headed in the same direction they traveled. An uncostumed bodyguard limping ahead of a woman in Western wear probably attracted plenty of watchful eyes from the surrounding aliens, mythical creatures, and otherwise oddly dressed throng.

As they approached the assigned room, Carlton spotted a line of costumed fans snaking from the water fountain near the door and doubling back and forth in front of the hall. A few of them waved at his client. A couple of teen girls squealed and held their hands over their hearts as several celebrities filed in ahead of them. He glanced at the fans. No one appeared too suspicious, if he ignored the strange clothes. When they reached the door, Mara Shore stepped around him and held up her lanyard containing a bright orange name tag.

The host standing at the door waved her inside after checking her badge. "Welcome, Miss Shore. I love the humor in your comic strips. I'm apologizing to all our celebrities for the inconvenience of having to walk through the crowds. We found out too late that a back entrance wasn't available for this event due to behind-the-scenes renovations."

"This is my first comic convention, so I didn't realize that kind of service was available. Thank you for your apologies."

The young man nodded as he stared at Mara. "Your table is along the back wall."

If the guy had been a dog he would have drooled. Carlton bit back a grin.

"Thank you, sir. My bodyguard will be accompanying me." The sudden strength in her voice brooked no objections. The woman had grown some spunk now that they were out of the throngs.

Carlton watched the fellow's eyebrows rise when Mara mentioned the presence of a bodyguard, but he kept smiling while directing them into the room. Carlton followed her past a stand of people ready to sell tickets for each author's autographs. Then they headed toward a table sitting along the room's back wall.

Her steps became more confident than when she'd attempted to push through the crowd. A banner bearing her name and a large reproduction of a comic strip mule adorned the wall behind her chair. Thin permanent markers sat in cups on each table, ready for autographing. Several small packs of scratch pads lay nearby. Carlton guessed they had their purpose, but had no idea about their use at the moment.

He stepped behind her table, nodding to the fellow seated next to them. The guy wearing a futuristic law enforcement costume was vaguely familiar. When he extended his hand, Carlton shook it and recognition hit him. He'd seen the actor on a streaming show he'd watched. Carlton had seen most of the series while recovering from the second wound, making his use of a cane a requirement.

"It's nice to meet you in person. I enjoy your show." His greeting felt lame. At least he didn't drool.

"Are you autographing today?" Rodney Stone, who played Sergeant Packard on the crime series, nodded to where Mara was busy placing bookmarks and mule drawings in stacks.

"No. I'm former law enforcement. I'm here with Mara Shore as her bodyguard." Carlton waved a hand toward the woman. The western hat still obscured most of her face, but color rose on her neck. She didn't look happy. "I better see to my duties." He stepped closer to Mara while Rodney returned to his seat.

Mara's hands went to her hips. She whipped the hat off her head and ran fingers through wisps of ebony hair, pushing the errant strands back into her braid. She glared at him with glinting brown eyes and a wrinkled brow. "Look here, mister, I'm not paying you to be a fan boy. I need you watching for trouble."

"Yes, ma'am." Her timid personality no longer remained. Carlton lifted his free hand in a mock salute and took a stance behind her chair. "I'm at your service."

"Good." She paused for a heartbeat as she swiveled to face him. Her expression softened. "Sorry I snapped. It's been a long tour, one I didn't want to do. My agent insisted even though..."

Her unfinished sentence reminded Carlton of the threatening texts she'd supposedly received. Unfortunately, by the time Mara decided to contact Guardians Security the messages no longer existed on her phone. "I understand, Miss Shore."

Carlton wasn't totally convinced of a serious threat. Most likely the messages were the prank of an obsessed fan wanting their five minutes of fame. He'd accepted the assignment despite his disbelief of her fears and strong dislike of mules, since one of the critters had injured him for life. Keeping her safe was his first case since resigning from his government job and joining the newly formed security group. The bottom line was he needed the income to pay bills not covered by insurance. He would do the best job he could for her.

"Do you suspect anyone in this room?"

"Not really, but at this point I don't know who is making the threats." She fingered the rim of her felt hat before setting it back on her head. This time it rested farther back, revealing her concerned expression.

He searched her heart-shaped face. Long lashes encircled her wide brown eyes. A slight blush adorned high cheekbones. Pink lips tightened in a grimace. Worry lines marred her forehead and touched his doubting soul.

He nodded and turned to study the room. The autographing participants all focused on getting their tables set up. Exit doors were clearly marked, each one manned by someone wearing a host badge on their lanyard.

"The room looks secure for now, Miss Shore. I promise to protect you if there's a threat from the fans."

"Thank you." She heaved a deep sigh and sat in her chair. Her eyes closed as she bowed her head. He wondered if she was praying. He used to pray all the time before the accident, before a mule ran him over and destroyed his career as a federal agent.

An announcement about the doors opening interrupted his thoughts. Fans swarmed into the room. After purchasing tickets, the eager crowd formed lines in front of each celebrity. Large mule ears attached to headbands decorated several of the people headed toward his client's table. It looked like the only threat at the moment might be a stubborn mule fan.

Mara straightened in her chair and pasted on what looked like a forced smile. A mother and two young mule-eared fans approached her with their mouths hanging open. The older girl placed a bright green ticket and a book on the table as she danced from one foot to the other.

~~~~~

"Hi, Miss Shore. Will you sign our book?" Mule ears bobbed as the elementary-aged girl bounced next to a similar looking preschooler and a woman with the same hair color.

Leah Beach, aka Mara Shore, nodded and picked up a pen. "Who would you like me to address the autograph to?" She pushed a marker and pad of scratch paper to the mother and asked for the correct spelling of the girls' names. Leah's smile became genuine as she spoke with the little family and enjoyed their chatter. Maybe one day she'd have a family of her own.

That would take meeting someone. Her loner lifestyle didn't offer many contacts with unmarried men. For a second she wondered about Carlton's married status. He didn't look much older than her twenty-seven years. She shook that thought off and concentrated on the task at hand.

Using her author's pseudonym grated on her conscience as she reached for the graphic novel that had started this tour across the country. The assumed name separated her from riding on Daddy's coattails as a way to fame, a choice she'd made for that purpose. Her thoughts wandered as she scrawled a dedication to Gracie and Mae before signing her pen name. The scent of permanent marker tickled the
~~~~~

inside of her nose. She managed to stifle a sneeze.

Leah had been content with her syndicated comic strip until her agent convinced her to create an entire book based on her mule characters. She'd enjoyed writing and drawing in the new genre. However, the task of publicizing the graphic novel was tearing Leah away from her typical days of ranching and creating in private.

Penny Barrington, her agent, was already pushing for the completion of her second graphic novel. The first was a top-seller and had received glowing reviews in New York and Chicago. The extra income had grown more important to Penny in recent months. The agent's obsession with the increased income often grated on Leah's nerves, even though she appreciated having the additional funds to help support her mule rescue ranch.

An hour flew by as Leah signed book after book with her Mara Shore moniker. Fans of her comic strip brought colorful clippings from Sunday papers. She laughed with admirers as they perused *Marty the Mule's Musings*.

Several expressed interest in the latest addition of Sylvester the Appaloosa mule. She'd modeled her drawings of the long-eared equine after the latest acquisition at the mule rescue. The poor beast had come to the ranch in a starved condition. His hooves were in bad shape when he arrived from an auction house. In the last week, he needed special treatments to cure an infection. The heart-shaped spots on his rump inspired the addition of Sylvester's character for the comic strip.

During a short lull, Carlton laid a hand on her shoulder. A hint of mossy aftershave made her more aware of his proximity. Warmth coursed through her body. She really needed to get out more, or maybe stay away from any man that could send that kind of jolt through her body. It didn't help that the hunk looked like a weightlifter and had gorgeous green eyes.

He smiled down at her, pushing a hank of wavy brown hair to one side. "I've learned a lot about your mules and comics today. You've got great fans too. Is there anything I can get for you?"

Her mouth felt dry. "Maybe refill my water bottle."

He reached for the container as she held it up to him. His touch sent a shiver through her body.

"Are you cold?" His voice was smooth and mellow.

She shook her stiff fingers out as she hunted for an answer that didn't make her look foolish. "No. I'm just jittery from everything." She looked away for a moment, but her gaze trailed his movement as he turned and wove his way toward the door. Refocusing, she spotted a couple of teen boys approaching her table.

"Hi, guys. I'm so glad you came to see me."

Spots of pink covered the boys' cheeks as they elbowed each other and stuttered out a few words about the graphic novel. Their cowboy attire attested to their curiosity about ranching.

"Does your interest in *Marty the Mule's Musings* have anything to do with an actual experience with mules or ranching?"

The shorter young man's shoulders relaxed. "We don't have any mules on our farm, but we do have a donkey. He gets in trouble all the time. Your mule stories remind us of Zeke."

Leah laughed and signed their copy of a comic strip along with two bookmarks. Her line had grown again while they spoke. A frowning man dressed as a pharaoh stood behind the boys.

The guy was the one she'd noticed earlier. Where was her bodyguard? It shouldn't take that long to fill her water bottle. She looked up at the pharaoh as he stepped forward. A mask covered most of his face. He slapped down a comic strip featuring her newest character, Sylvester the Appaloosa mule.

"Where did you find this mule?" His voice rasped like a smoker's as he pointed to her rendering of the spotted mule.

"I created him for my comic strip." She wasn't about to reveal that Sylvester was modeled from a real mule housed at her rescue facility.

"Look, lady, I don't mean your silly little ink drawings. The markings on this animal are exactly like a mule that wandered off from our operation a while ago. We need him back. I think you stole him." The man hovered close enough for her to smell onions and lingering tobacco on his breath.

Leah leaned back and held a hand to her nose. This type of threat was one she'd hoped to avoid by having a bodyguard nearby.

"What's going on here?" Her nerves calmed as Carlton plunked down her water bottle and placed a hand on the man's elbow. Her guardian pulled the costumed pharaoh back a step from her table.

Leah's water bottle rolled across the table from where Carlton had dropped it. She grabbed the container and then pointed a shaking hand toward the stranger. "He was getting too pushy about one of the mules in *Marty the Mule's Musings*."

"She knows where my animal is, and I want it back." The man glared at her as Carlton continued to hold his arm.

Leah noted Carlton's raised eyebrows and decided to clarify the situation. "This guy thinks I have his mule. My comic strip character, Sylvester, resembles one he claims ran away from him." She pointed to the comic strip lying where the stranger had slapped it down. Carlton frowned.

Self-inflicted pain stung her jaw as she clamped it shut, refusing to reveal that there might be some truth to the man's claim. If the stranger did own the mule, animal abuse authorities would have something to say about the sickly animal she'd taken in. They had worked hard with Sylvester when it came to dealing with a consuming fear of small places, including barns and stalls.

She watched Carlton squint as he picked up the comic with his free hand and glanced between her and the pharaoh. Did he know she wasn't sharing the whole truth? "Are you sure about this, mister?" Carlton glared at the Egyptian-clad character.

A crowd had gathered around them. The futuristic cop actor, Rodney Stone, rose from his autograph table and now stood next to her.

She frowned at the pharaoh. "Give me your name and address, and I'll let you know if I discover anything about your mule." Leah dared the man to share his information. She'd make sure he paid for the damage done to Sylvester if there was a connection.

The man in Carlton's grasp stopped struggling. "Never mind, lady. Maybe I'm wrong." He shrugged out of Carlton's grip. Glaring eyes met hers as the masked pharaoh muttered under his breath, "But I don't think so." Turning, he pushed through the crowded room.

She watched as Carlton's gaze followed the man's retreating figure until the pharaoh stepped from the room. Then he took his position behind her without speaking. She saw him stuff the pharaoh's crumpled comic into his pocket.

A shiver shook Leah's composure. Her hired bodyguard wasn't happy. Neither was she. Regret about going on this tour in the first place made her angry. If a longtime benefactor for the rescue ranch hadn't recently pulled their support, she never would have agreed to go on the road with her book. At least the journey would be over after one more event following this convention.

A few fans still remained in her line. Focusing on their joy at meeting the creator of Marty the mule helped her make it through the rest of the signing. Most people brought copies of the new graphic novel for her autograph. Tension released from her shoulders when the last fans headed for the doors.

At least the books sold well. That should help both the ranch and satisfy her aggressive agent, Penny. The woman promised to be with her at the convention but hadn't shown up for the autograph session. At least Penny came earlier to set up the book banner. Her absence seemed odd. She'd been like a pesky buzzard circling Leah for killer sales during all the other events.

From the time Penny signed on as Leah's agent, they'd had a cordial relationship. However, during the last few months, strain had risen between the two women. Penny pushed for more paying public opportunities. Those activities had stretched Leah's private lifestyle to the maximum and overwhelmed her creativity with book deadlines piled on top of daily comic strip demands. A second graphic novel was already in the works, but the time needed for multiple illustrations per page would take another year before completion. Penny kept asking for a closer deadline.

After the doors closed on the last straggling fans, Leah picked up leftover Mara Shore and Marty the Mule bookmarks. She placed them in a folder she transferred into her backpack. When she reached for the banner, Carlton took the other end and helped her take it down. Their hands touched as they reached the final fold. She snatched the material from him and pushed it into the backpack, careful not to snag the hanging on the electronic tablet, pencils, and sketch pad she always kept handy in her bag. His touch bothered her in a pleasant way, one she didn't have the experience to pursue.

Drawing the comic strip had always been her passion, along with caring for mules in need of a good home. Too often the long-ears ended up permanently staying on her ranch. Creating the graphic novel had, at first, provided an interesting experience. Now it felt like a chore. The pressure to create more books in the genre wasn't as appealing to her anymore, not when deadlines pushed into the things she enjoyed and placed danger in her path. She had initially liked Penny, but maybe it was time to start thinking about a different agent.

Chapter Two

Carlton's attention strayed to the throng hovering outside the main exit doors, which still stood partially open. The costumed mummy, who'd asked him for directions when he'd topped off his client's water bottle, stood near the opening. The wrapped character placed one of his draped arms around the threatening pharaoh character and shook a finger in the man's face. The guy's delaying questions at the water fountain suddenly made sense. The distraction by the mummy had provided time for the man's partner in crime to threaten Miss Shore. Carlton couldn't fall for another ruse. Standing quietly on guard as she packed up her gear was the best he could do. He'd messed up by not taking her concerns seriously. Her safety needed all his concentration.

He stuffed one hand in his pocket. The commandeered comic crinkled, reminding him of another dilemma. That issue was personal, and it might involve her speckled mule. The markings on the mule were too familiar. That made him wonder if that had anything to do with Kent choosing him for the assignment. His boss wanted him to forgive the past and move on. Was this a ploy to make him face the mule that sealed his fate? One of the other Guardians employees loved riding as much as he did. Cara would have enjoyed the assignment.

"I'm ready when you are." Mara's wavering voice broke into his thoughts.

"It looks like the threat has moved on for now. You have my full attention." Carlton hoped that would suffice as an apology.

She shuddered. "Good." Shouldering her pack, she edged toward one of the side exit doors. "Just get me out of here and back to my hotel room in one piece. After that, I plan for us to part ways."

Her frown pierced his confidence. The Guardians Security Group contract went through the rest of the weekend. Dismissal from his first assignment wouldn't go over well with his new employer, even though they were friends and former co-workers.

"What about your other book signing?"

"I'm going to ask my agent to cancel the last event. If she won't, then there must be a capable employee in your group who can fulfill the protection duties for a day." Her gaze swept from his wounded leg up to stare at his face.

That stung. He wanted to protest. Instead, he tamped down his pride and offered her the apology she deserved. "Look, I'm sorry I didn't realize how serious this was. That won't happen again. I realize the threat is real and promise to be on guard for the rest of your tour."

"We'll see." She started to push through the exit door opening.

Carlton stepped forward. "At least let me do my job for today." He held up a hand and slowly opened the door the rest of the way. Peering out into the crowded hallway, he searched for the mummy and pharaoh. They weren't in sight. He motioned her out into the throng. "Follow me. I'll take you back to the hotel."

Once again, he felt her fingers tug on the back of his shirt as they pushed through the masses. The quickest way to the attached hotel meant heading across the exhibit hall full of publishers, advertisers, and characters promoting television, movies, books, or other media. Tapping his cane helped open a path through the thickening swarm of strangers. The smell of sweaty bodies wafted through the air. The scent had gotten stronger as the day took its toll on costumed people. Her grip on his shirt pulled from one side to the other as he pushed through the large gathering place. The brim of her hat bumped into his back, keeping him aware of her presence.

Looking over his shoulder, he took note that the vacuum he'd created closed as soon as they passed through. For the moment, no signs of the Egyptian characters emerged. He made his way to one side of the room and spotted an opening behind someone in a bobbing blow-up dinosaur costume. Following the creature's tail made it easier to travel forward.

"Are you doing all right back there?" Carlton swiveled his head to look at her and survey the milling crowd once more.

Her grasp on his shirt loosened and fell away. "I've been better. At least I can breathe now." She took a step forward as they walked side-by-side in the wake of the giant reptile's swishing tail. "Are you sure you know how to get to the hotel from here?"

"I studied the layout before coming." He clamped his mouth shut to avoid saying more about how he knew the quickest way to their destination. She'd made it clear she didn't believe him capable of keeping her safe. His clumping cane reminded him of his own failings. If he'd made a different decision in the past, or never had a close encounter with a mule, there'd be no need for a cane. He'd still be a federal agent.

Carlton glanced at the crowd one more time. There were no Egyptians on the crowded side of the room or in a booth. Suddenly, the dinosaur in front veered into an open area where the costumed person joined several other prehistoric beasts. The crowd closed in again, revealing the mummy and pharaoh coming straight toward them.

Carlton grabbed Leah's arm at the same time the mummy latched onto her other side.

"She's coming with me unless she wants to tell where to find our missing mule." The low-pitched threatening voice reached Carlton's ears. He recognized it as the one belonging to the man who'd delayed him earlier. This time the mummy would not take advantage of him.

Lifting his cane, Carlton brought it down on the mummy's forearm with a thump. Even though the wrapping on the man's arm provided some protection, the impact was enough to loosen the villain's grip.

The pharaoh slipped forward to take his companion's place. Light reflected off a white porcelain knife in his hand. He grabbed her shoulder and lifted the blade. Carlton's cane caught the weapon on an upward swing. The knife flew into the throng. People screamed. The crowd parted as the knife crashed on the floor. Security guards fought to make their way through the panic.

The Egyptian-clad pair disappeared into the crowd. Carlton moved Leah behind him, sandwiching her between the wall and his body. He stood his ground until the convention center security guards reached them. Carlton recognized Mark Wakefield, an off-duty policeman. The lawman bagged the broken knife as evidence and began taking their statements.

"Do you know of any reason why these men want your mule, Miss Shore?" The officer held a small pad of paper for taking notes.

"I have no idea. If you do catch them, someone needs to accuse them of animal cruelty. The poor creature was nearly dead when I found him at an auction. I'm glad for your presence at the event." She glanced sideways and down at her feet before meeting Carlton's gaze. "And I'm glad I hired a bodyguard to accompany me."

Carlton lowered his shoulders as tension drained from them. He hoped he had redeemed himself by his actions.

The policeman clapped a hand on Carlton's shoulder. "He's a good guy. Carlton and I trained together at the police academy before he headed off to be a Fed. Sorry to hear your injury took you out of commission with your government job."

The officer looked down at the cane, then back up at Miss Shore. "Guardians Security Group is blessed to have him. He'll take good care of you. In the meantime, I've let all the convention hall security guards know about the two Egyptian characters that attacked you, Miss Shore. I do have to warn you that I've seen at least a dozen people in similar outfits. It might be difficult to locate the ones who harassed you."

"Thanks for your help, Officer Wakefield. Please let us know if you find anything." Carlton and Mark had been friends during their training days and before, when they'd met as orphaned twelve-year-old kids. After law enforcement training, they'd headed off to different places to serve, and the close connection had been lost with the exception of an occasional Christmas message. He shook the man's hand. "Maybe we can touch base again soon."

Mark's handclasp tightened as a smile crossed his face. "Sounds good, Cowboy."

"Cowboy?" Miss Shore raised an eyebrow.

"That's a story for another day. Let's head for your hotel room, unless Officer Greenhorn has more questions for us." Carlton decided to share his friend's nickname too.

Mark laughed. "I don't have any other official questions. I'd be glad to follow you to her room, if you'd like."

"I think we're good. Let's share phone numbers though." Carlton exchanged business cards with his old friend. Maybe they could get together once his duties to Miss Shore were finished. He missed Mark and looked forward to reconnecting. "I can see the entrance to the hotel from here. Once we're in an elevator there shouldn't be a threat."

~~~~~

Leah crossed her arms. She'd hoped Officer Wakefield would accompany them to the hotel. She didn't like hearing "something *shouldn't* be a threat." Those words provided no guarantee of safety. Long ago, she'd told her famous dad that he shouldn't worry about the one boyfriend she'd dated in her lifetime. Things had totally gone wrong when the guy kidnapped her and started demanding money from her wealthy parent. Maybe it was happening again with these Egyptian creepers, only Daddy wasn't going to rescue her this time because of her stubbornness and his.

"Are you coming?" Carlton's voice interrupted her thoughts. He reached toward her.

She ignored his offered hand and stomped toward the hotel. Dad once told her she was as stubborn as one of her mules. Maybe he was right. An elevator door opened and she ran for the empty car. She tapped her hotel room card on the scanner and began entering her floor number. The door started closing as Carlton hobbled closer. Fighting the temptation to leave him behind, she hit the open door button at the same time his cane pushed between the closing panels.

"I'm still on the job. Let me see you to your room." Carlton's frustration filled the elevator car as he stepped inside.

Something else lingered in the small space. Could she be imagining the scent of onions and cigarettes? She sniffed the air.

Carlton inhaled and frowned. "This elevator stinks like an onion-
~~~~~

eating smoker. I think I caught a similar smell on our pharaoh when he attacked."

"Were they coming from the hotel when they came at us?" Her voice shook.

"That's a possibility. Maybe they talked someone into taking them up, but the hotel shouldn't have given them your room number." Carlton tapped his cane on the elevator carpeting as the car rose.

"Please don't say 'shouldn't.' That word is not on my favorite word list." She put curled fists on her hips.

"We have to be prepared for anything." He edged closer to the doors as the elevator slowed. "I'll go first."

She didn't argue as she watched him lean out and then nod for her to follow. The stifling scent also lingered in the hall. Her door looked untouched. He took her card and waved it near the keypad. Unlocking sounds clicked and purred. Carlton opened the door and froze in place.

"What's wrong?" She pushed her way underneath his arm and stared at the clutter. Someone had trashed the room. The emptied bathroom and closets confirmed they'd come and gone. "No."

Carlton's hands gripped her shoulders for a second before she elbowed him away.

"You need to stay out of the room until we have Mark take a look."

She took two steps before his words made her move back into the hall. Leah slid to the floor. Disbelief chilled her from head to toe as she wrapped her arms across her chest and fought nausea. "I want to go home."

Carlton bent down next to her. "We'll arrange for your safety, but right now I need to call Officer Wakefield and get him to check out the room."

She closed her eyes and prayed for strength as she listened to him contact the policeman. Within a few minutes, Mark Wakefield and hotel security arrived. She pulled herself together while they searched.

Ten minutes later the policeman stepped from the room. "We've taken pictures and secured the room. Are you willing to come in and let us know if anything is missing? Also, if you have any idea how these people got into a locked room without a hotel key, I'd appreciate knowing what you think." Officer Wakefield stretched out his hand.

She took it and stood, releasing a huff. "I'll do my best to check for missing items. I don't have any idea about your question, other than letting you know my agent has a room key." Leah blinked back tears as she stared at the disaster. A sense of violation made her shiver. Clothing littered the room. A bag filled with markers and other art supplies she used for cartooning spilled from the desk and onto the floor beneath.

The latest comic strip she'd been working on lay torn in several pieces. The panel with Sylvester was either missing or ripped to shreds.

"I think it was the same guys. They tore Sylvester out of this comic strip. The pharaoh specifically mentioned my new Appaloosa mule and he's missing from this panel. I'll have to redo the piece before the morning deadline." She'd already asked for an extension since the Friday afternoon due date for the piece had passed by several hours.

The urgency to regroup and get the panel redone sent her to work. She gathered scraps of paper from the floor and desk and placed them in a heap. She glanced at Officer Wakefield. "May I pick up the pens or do you need to look for fingerprints?"

He shook his head. "I doubt we'll find any prints. Carlton said the costumed characters that attacked you were wearing gloves. It's pretty obvious they are the most likely culprits."

She hadn't noticed that detail. Carlton had, which was another point in his favor, not that she would need him after she canceled Saturday's book signing at a mall. "Excuse me, I need to call my agent and take care of a few details concerning tomorrow." She collapsed in the desk chair and put her phone on speaker. While she waited for an answer, she smoothed the torn pieces and tried patching them together on the desktop. Sylvester was definitely not in the picture.

"Hello, Mara darling. How can I help?" The agent's voice grated on Leah's tattered nerves as she tried to steady her voice.

"Hey, Penny. I need to cancel tomorrow's event at the mall bookstore."

"Whatever for?"

"Someone broke into my room, destroyed this week's comic strip, and scattered my belongings all over the place. I've been threatened, physically mauled, and the police need to know where your key to this room is right now." Leah forced air into her lungs, glad she'd managed to sound forceful for the few sentences she spewed out.

"The police?" Penny cleared her throat. Rustling crackled in the background. "I... I can't find it in my purse. I dropped my bag when someone bumped into me after I set up your banner this morning."

"Well, someone found or took it. I don't feel safe. I want out of this hotel and out of tomorrow's autograph session."

"Sorry, Mara. You signed a contract. You need to honor your commitment to the tour contract and your obligations to the publishers." This time the agent's stringent tones were insistent with no room for an argument. "You're the one who hired a bodyguard. Let them keep you safe for the event. I wish you'd asked my advice on that decision rather than hiring some unknown security company."

Leah huffed. She was tired of being Mara. She wanted to head home, but if she went home, she'd miss out on a large portion of the money from tour sales. Penny's words had reminded her of a clause in the contract. Her mules needed her support. "Can you at least get me a safer place to stay the night?"

"I might be able to locate something. Give me a few minutes. I'll see what I can do." The confident agent's professional voice had returned.

"I'll need an internet connection to get my comic to Media Sources by morning."

"Understood. I'll get back to you in a few minutes." Penny ended the phone connection.

Leah gathered her art materials and started reworking *Marty Mule's Musings* latest comic strip adventure.

The policeman and Carlton stood talking at the door. They both turned and stared in her direction.

"Is there a problem, gentlemen?" Having the eyes of both men focused on her made Leah uncomfortable.

Carlton pointed to the clothing strewn across the carpeted floor. "You're welcome to put your clothes back in place so you'll be ready to move to a new location."

"I've got a deadline to meet. Clothes can wait. Mules can't. Maybe you fellows could make yourselves useful and pick up a few things for me while I do my job." Leah lifted her marker and glared.

Officer Wakefield grimaced. "I'll keep guard outside. She's your client, Cowboy."

Chapter Three

Carlton stared at the mess. He'd never dealt with women's clothing before. Mrs. Dudley, the woman who took on the role of mother to the guys he'd grown up with at the boys' ranch, had never asked any of the fellows to deal with her clothing. Mr. and Mrs. Dudley's home was for boys only, until Carlton's older sister discovered she had a brother.

Tamera came on board to cook for the growing population of males while Mrs. Dudley recovered from an operation. Eventually, his sister helped the older couple manage the ranch home during his last year there. Other than the girls at school, who'd mostly ignored the crew of orphan boys, his life had centered on his all-male home life until after high school graduation. During police training there'd only been a few women, all of them wearing the same basic clothing as the men and they'd done their own sorting and cleaning.

Being in law enforcement had consumed his life, leaving little time for dating. He hadn't been particularly interested in pursuing a relationship after seeing several of his colleagues endure divorces from work-related stress in their marriages. His own attempt at romance had ended in a disaster and even his ex-girlfriend had never asked him to help with her laundry.

"Are you sure you want me dealing with all your clothing?" Heat blistered his cheeks.

She gave him an odd look, then grinned. "Just do what I asked. I know it isn't in the job description, but I need to get this comic finished before morning. Just in case Penny doesn't find us a more secure place to stay with internet, I'd like to get this completed before we leave here." She turned her back and resumed working on the art.

"I'll do what I can." He pushed everything into a pile with his cane and began to awkwardly scoop the clothing onto a bed with one hand. He picked up a pair of slacks, shook them out and gave them a precision folding. Tee shirts came next. Those were things he could handle. He caught Mara glancing his way as he stacked the items into her suitcase. A few fancy tops and her unmentionables remained.

"Do you think I've done enough?" He sure thought so.

She actually laughed. "Thank you for doing a nice job with my pants and tops. Where did you learn to fold clothes so perfectly?" She held a pen poised over lightly sketched pencil marks on the restarted comic.

"I lived on a boys' ranch after I turned twelve. The house parents provided us with a loving Christian environment, but they expected us to learn self-discipline. Keeping our clothes in order was part of their training." He took a few steps closer to look over her shoulder.

Her pen strokes agilely covered the rough pencil marks and brought out the adventurous mules' personalities. She blew on the ink and then pulled an eraser from her backpack.

"Is the boys' ranch where you got the nickname, Cowboy?" Mara started erasing pencil lines not covered in ink.

"Yeah. Mark came there not long after me. He didn't have much experience with horses, but I did. I called him Greenhorn. He decided if he was Greenhorn, then I had to be Cowboy."

"Where did you learn about riding?" She blew erasure debris from the drawing.

"My single mother was part of a rodeo circuit. When she died, the authorities couldn't find anyone else to claim me or her elderly horse. The ranch made perfect sense as a living space for me and Mom's old mare. Wind Catcher only made it a few years after arriving at the ranch, but I was happy they didn't separate us. She's buried in the horse cemetery on that property." He cleared his throat. "What about you? When did you start taking in mules?"

"I always rode my parents' horses until I went to a mule event. Those creatures' long ears and sassy ways inspired me to start making *Marty the Mule's Musings*. To be authentic, I went shopping and found the perfect mule to model Marty after. He'd trained for trail riding, so I shifted my riding skills over to his back. What an amazing mount. His former owner called him Smarty Pants. It wasn't long before he began answering to Marty. When I heard about abused mules, I decided to start a rescue ranch. I'm not sure I'll ever go back to riding horses again."

"I'm glad I ride horses. I don't like ornery animals and don't have much respect for mules after..."

"I've met plenty of ornery horses and horsemen," she interrupted, and blew out a horse snort between her lips. Then she lifted an electronic tablet out of her backpack and held it above the comic strip. He heard the click as she snapped a photo.

"What are you going to do now?" Carlton moved closer to peer over her shoulder at the drawing.

"I'm going to drop the picture into a digital drawing app on my electronic tablet. I can clean up any flaws I haven't fixed and then send it out into cyber space. After that, I'm done until Monday. My syndication contract doesn't have obligations over the weekend."

"Aren't you cutting your deadlines a little close?" He watched as she tapped in several commands and then used a stylus to touch up her work.

"Normally I'd work a couple of weeks ahead, but this tour has pushed my schedule out of whack." Using two fingers, she twisted the picture this way and that as she erased, enlarged, and made different marks. Then she held the tablet up so he could see the comic. "What do you think?"

"You're quite the artist. I'll have to start checking out your comic strip."

"So you aren't one of my top fans?" She raised her dark eyebrows.

"I've been busy trying to keep the world safe from the bad guys and ornery mules. I don't usually waste time on unnecessary pursuits."

She glared at him. "Based on your earlier body language, I'm thinking you thought my case was a waste of your time until an actual threat occurred, Cowboy."

"You nailed it, Miss Shore. I'm sorry I didn't take you seriously until then."

"Call me Mara, or even better, call me Leah. I'm sure they let you know my real name when you took the case."

"Yes, ma'am."

She raised an eyebrow.

"I mean yes, Leah."

"Now that we've straightened out a few things, and I can't get out of the final tour date, I won't break your contract either."

"Thanks. I appreciate your vote of confidence." He really did. Confidence wasn't his constant companion since his crippling event.

"So, will you actually read my comic strip and tell me what you think before I send it in?" She held out the tablet.

Her face begged for his approval. He couldn't help noticing the glow of excitement as she shared her finished product. The worried woman from the comic convention had transformed into a beautiful artist wanting to share her work.

He took the tablet from her hand. The drawings and the message made him chuckle, something he hadn't done in a long time. "I like it. You did a fine job, Leah." He looked up from the tablet and focused on her face. "You have a nice name. Why hide behind a pseudonym?"

She took the tablet back, perused it, and tapped more commands. A whooshing sound indicated she'd sent the file. Her lips pursed and then tugged inwards before she answered his question. "My dad is a very famous cartoonist. He lives in the spotlight. Dad's characters have been in movies, on television, and featured in video games, in addition to daily comic strips. I didn't want to ride into the industry as Leonardo Beach's daughter."

"Wow. I still have a collection of Leonardo Beach's cartoon figurines that Mom bought me when she was alive." Carlton couldn't believe he'd missed the connection. Memories overtook his thoughts.

"Your fan-boy reaction is exactly why I use a pen name. Living in the public eye and dealing with Dad's dominance was not fun." Bitterness leaked from Leah's words.

"Do you think someone is trying to harass you because of that connection?"

"Not this time." She shook her head.

"What do you mean by 'this time'?" Curiosity and a vague memory from the past filtered into his thoughts.

"That's another discussion for another day. I hired you because of the threatening messages I've been receiving. The Egyptian man clearly stated he wanted to find my latest rescue mule, Sylvester. He must be the one trying to harass me. I'm guessing he abused the poor animal and is afraid I'm going to hand his information over to the authorities. Maybe he should be running from us. If I ever do get his information, I will turn that man in. Sylvester already has a case started with a cruelty to animals agency."

"Did your newest mule happen to run away during a federal sting that took place six months ago?" Carlton rubbed his aching leg.

A knock on the door halted their conversation. Carlton looked through the peephole. Mark stood outside with a woman dressed in a business pantsuit. She was shaking a finger at him as her red lips moved. Carlton assumed the female was Miss Shore's agent, but caution overrode trust. "What does your agent look like?"

"She's blonde, around my height, and usually wears bright red lipstick." Frustration laced Leah's voice.

"It looks like she's here. Would you like me to let her in?" After Leah's nod, he opened the door.

Mark looked relieved to send the chatty woman inside. "Hey, Cowboy. I'm off duty from the convention center. I've got to go get some sleep before my regular police shift in the morning. Call me if you need anything."

"Thanks. Hopefully we're done with the excitement for now." Carlton's time with Leah had technically ended for the evening too. The Guardians Security Group contract didn't call for overnight duty, but since the threat was real he didn't want to leave Leah without a guard. Noting that the two frowning women had busied themselves with the rest of the packing, he texted his boss a quick message about staying nearby overnight.

Kent returned his message immediately. *No problem. Do what you feel is necessary. Call for reinforcements as needed.*

I'm good for now. Carlton pocketed his phone and turned his attention to the two fussing females.

"I don't want to stay another night in this hotel. Those guys obviously know the location of the room I'm in since they busted in before." Leah snapped her suitcase closed and stood with hands on hips.

The agent matched Leah's position and glared. "The hotel is sorry about that and has offered a private suite on another floor for free."

"A free room should make you happy, Penny." Leah started shoving art materials into a small bag that she stuffed into her backpack. "I didn't think there were any vacancies here. I was hoping we could leave this hotel."

Penny lifted her chin. "Someone left the convention early and the suite room opened up. They are cleaning it as we speak. We can move you there as soon as the maids finish changing sheets. It's the best I can do at the last moment. You'll still have the internet connection to make your deadline."

"That's not an issue since I just sent my assignment in." Leah crossed her arms.

Penny matched her defiant stand. "I don't have any secure options open locally. This city is hosting two major conferences, and there's nothing available except the suite." She took the handle of Leah's suitcase and pointed her toward the door.

Carlton cleared his throat. "If the location is a suite, it has more than one bedroom. I just got the okay from my boss at the Guardians Security Group to stay on duty overnight. Miss Shore can lock herself in a room, and I'll sleep by the door."

Both women scowled at him. He shrugged. "Penny could use the other bed if that makes you ladies feel more secure. I'll still hang out at the door."

Penny shook her head. "I will stay in my personal accommodations. Mara can make her own choice, but I'm sure the hotel will secure her privacy tonight." Her phone pinged with a message. She read it and looked up. "Suite 1240 is ready. A staff member will be waiting with your keycards."

He watched Leah frown as her shoulders lowered. She lifted her backpack into place and pulled the handle of her rolling suitcase from Penny's grip. "I don't like sharing my space, but based on the threats, I will accept Carlton's offer as long as he leaves me alone."

Carlton had no plans to bother her. "You have my word. Keeping you from harm is my job and only goal." He held his palms up before waving her toward the door.

They proceeded to the elevators. Penny left them when an elevator car going down arrived. An upward-bound one came seconds later and they headed to the suite.

As promised, a maid handed over their key cards. She introduced them to a uniformed hotel security guard who had stationed a chair in the hallway. "This is Andrew. He will be standing guard through the night if you like."

"I would like that." Leah nodded to the man.

"I'll be here all night, Miss." The guard saluted. "We are very sorry for the violation of your privacy earlier."

"Thank you, Andrew. We'll keep her safe between the two of us." Carlton shook the security guard's hand and closed the door after they entered. He twisted the deadbolt and flipped the metal door guard in place. When he turned to speak to Leah, she was closing the door to one of the bedrooms. "Is everything secure in there? I wanted to check before you turned in for the night."

She opened the door a crack. "The only person in here is me."

"Do me a favor. Check the bathroom and then let me know you're good." He pushed the door open another inch and watched her do as he'd requested.

"I'm good. Now, if you don't mind, I'm heading to bed." She slammed the door shut. He heard the lock click and then checked out the rest of the suite. All was in order. The fresh scent of sanitizer made him sneeze. He often reacted to cleaning odors when they entered his nose.

A muffled "Bless you" came from Leah through the closed door.

"Thank you, sweet dreams."

"I hope so." Tiredness leaked from her voice.

"I'll be praying for you." His response came without thinking. He hoped God would hear his prayers. He whispered a prayer for forgiveness for his lack of communication with his creator, before petitioning for Leah to have a good night.

Carlton looked around the room and decided to slide the suite's recliner near the door. Moving the chair proved awkward because of his limping leg, but he managed. *Please Lord, help me to perform this job, despite my disability.* After he'd wiggled the easy chair into position, he took a blanket from the extra bed and settled in, hoping to rest as much as he could for the remainder of the night. He turned the hotel lamps off and noticed light still showing from the crack beneath Leah's door. Carlton pulled the cover over his head and leaned the recliner back. His eyes closed as he let weariness claim his tired body.

Hours later, a thump startled him awake. He raised the recliner to a seated position and leaned over to look out the peephole. His hand reached for his side where no weapon existed. He'd not brought a sidearm to the convention due to the event's safety rules. His cane would have to do for now.

The scene outside the door didn't bode well. Two men in black clothes and ski masks were pulling Andrew down the hall. Carlton flipped on the lights and dialed the hotel desk. No one picked up. They were on their own. It wouldn't be long before the criminals broke in if the guard possessed a master keycard. He rapped on Leah's door. "Get your clothes on. We may need to make a run for it."

"I slept in my clothes. I'll be right out." The door opened. She stepped from the room with her backpack on, slipping one foot into a shoe. "What's the plan?"

"There are two of them again. They've taken out the guard. If Andrew had a passkey, they'll be coming in soon."

"What about the deadbolt?"

"It would depend on what type of key Andrew has. Leave the light on in your room. Partially close the door. Then stand behind me. Call 911 and pray." Carlton pushed the recliner to the side and turned off the lights after they were in position. "If they get inside, run for the stairs and don't stop until you get help at the front desk. I'll fight them for as long as I can, then follow if I'm able."

Leah's phone lit the darkness as she contacted 911 and explained the situation. "I'll keep my phone on, but I'm going to put it in my pocket for now."

Carlton felt her breath on the back of his neck as she leaned closer. He didn't need the distraction. "Take a step back. I'm going to need to swing my cane."

Darkness encompassed the space until the whir of the master key working on the lock broke the silence. It looked like they weren't safe. Carlton poised his cane for a low sweep. The sound of splintering wood indicated the deadbolt and metal guard would soon give way to the person battering the door open.

Chapter Four

Leah stepped back as Carlton positioned his cane parallel to the floor, ready to swing. She shifted her backpack to a more comfortable position, preparing for her run to the stairs. The idea of leaving Carlton alone to fight in her place didn't sit well with her conscience. She reached back to a side pocket on her bag and fisted a recently sharpened pencil. She'd learned a few things about self-defense, mostly on television shows, but she'd do what she could before sprinting for the stairwell.

The door cracked open. The metal clip on the door held during the first pounding, then fell to the floor as the perpetrators forced their way in. The first man in glanced toward her partially open door and pointed. Both men headed toward the light. Carlton's cane swung, knocking them down like bowling pins. They sprang to their feet and turned as Carlton took another swing at them.

"Run." He stepped out of her way and began punching at the two men. His cane thumped down to the carpeted floor. One of the men grabbed him from behind. The other approached with a raised fist.

Leah tightened her fingers around the pencil and stabbed at the man's shoulder. He fell to the floor screaming in pain.

Carlton swung his elbow back into the other man's side and shoved him away. "I told you to run."

"Not without my bodyguard."

He pushed his man to the ground. The guy's head bumped off the edge of a table. Carlton retrieved his cane. "Then we both better run before these guys are back on their feet."

"Ma'am, are you okay?" The sound came from her pocket. A 911 operator was still on the phone.

"We're leaving two injured bad guys in the suite. My bodyguard and I are heading for the stairs and hoping they aren't following." She shoved open the exit and waited for Carlton to go through with a more pronounced limp. She hoped he hadn't reinjured whatever required the cane's use. She bolted down the stairs with him following at a slower pace. After going down a few floors, she opened another door. "Let's catch an elevator from here."

"Sounds like a plan." Carlton followed her into an empty corridor and pushed the down button. "Step around the corner. If for some reason they're in the elevator, head back to the stairs."

Leah's legs trembled as she waited. *Ding*. An elevator arrived. She poked her head around the side wall and swallowed. She watched Carlton's expression as the door opened. He stepped halfway in and nodded for her to join him. Once inside he handed her a set of keys. "I've got a dark blue SUV parked in slot 268, right beside the bank of elevators, level B. If something happens after we get to the lobby, go to the garage and lock yourself in. If you don't hear from me in five minutes, drive away and don't look back. The GPS inside is set for Guardians headquarters. My boss has an apartment above the business. We can wait out the rest of the night there."

Leah watched the numbers count down as their elevator car headed for the lobby. When the door opened a chill rippled down her spine. Two men wearing black sat on a couch near the elevators. They no longer had their ski masks on but had pulled hoods from their sweatshirts over their heads, shadowing their faces. One tapped the other when the elevator doors parted.

Leah reached for the button closing the doors at the same time Carlton hit B2 for basement parking.

"My vehicle is right outside the elevator. Having a handicap parking sticker is at least worth something. Jump in as soon as you hit unlock." Carlton stepped close to the door as movement ceased.

She edged close to him. The door slid open slower than an obstinate mule. She hit the fob and heard a beep from his vehicle. She wedged her way out as soon as a space her size opened and headed for the SUV with the blinking lights. By the time she fastened her seatbelt, Carlton had climbed into the driver's seat and pushed a button to start the engine. He put his own belt on as he threw the car into reverse.

Leah stared in disbelief as the other elevator door opened and one of the men burst out, talking into a phone. She looked in the rearview mirror and watched the man run a few steps behind them, before stopping and lifting a fob that unlocked a nearby sedan.

"We've got a follower." She twisted in her seat and saw the man climbing into the dark car.

"I see. What kind of cash do you have on you?" Carlton wheeled around a corner in the parking garage.

"This isn't the time to be worried about your pay." She resisted rolling her eyes.

"I'm not thinking about my fee right now. A bribe might convince the garage attendant to delay this guy when we get out of here."

Leah pulled her backpack from where she'd tossed it on the floor and located several twenties in her wallet. "Will this do?" She waved the cash in the air.

"I hope so. Maybe we'll be blessed to have a fan of yours at the gate." Carlton rolled down his window as they approached the exit. He shoved his credit card in the slot to pay and then moved forward to chat with the attendant. He held up the twenties as they approached. "We've got a stalking fan harassing Miss Shore. He's in a dark sedan and should be coming up right behind us. Would you be willing to delay him for a bit? Here's a little extra for your trouble."

The young man waved away the bribe. "I would be glad to help Miss Shore. I love your new book. I'll take care of the stalker."

Leah gave him a smile and blew a fake kiss his way. "Thank you." She couldn't believe she'd done the pretend smooch, but neither could she comprehend all that had happened during the last few hours. She was so outside of her usual hermit ways.

As they pulled out into traffic, the other assailant came running around the corner of the building. The man ran in front of them with his fist raised in the air. Carlton swerved, nearly hitting an oncoming car. Leah gasped and grabbed the console and armrest as they rushed into the night.

~~~~~

Carlton's breath whooshed out of his chest. His heart beat fast, reliving the near miss with an innocent driver. Turning at the next corner, he concentrated on zigzagging toward the edge of the city. It wouldn't take long for the hoodlums to get their vehicle past the garage gatekeeper. If Carlton didn't follow a direct route to Forest Glen, they should be fine, unless the creeps had a way of tracking Leah. She'd only brought the backpack full of her art paraphernalia. He doubted any of her things held a tracker, but he needed to know for sure.

Once they reached the suburbs, he gave into his question. "Do me a favor and check your backpack for anything strange. I don't want anyone tracking us."

Leah pulled the bag closer and peered in. "I don't see anything right off. There are some sharp pencils that could be harmful to my hands if they're loose inside. Would you be able to stop somewhere where I can see better and won't be in danger of stabbing myself?"

"Sure." He rubbed his growling stomach.

She laughed. "We better make that a restaurant if you can find a place open at this time of night. I could use some protein and it sounds like you could too."

"Yeah. We both missed having an evening meal thanks to all our confrontations with the crooks. There's an all-night truck stop near the interstate. I'll swing closer to that road and hope our followers don't have the same idea, unless you want to have a protein bar from my desk at
~~~~~

work." Carlton drove the SUV toward the destination that would provide food and prayed they'd not meet with the crooks. About twenty minutes later he spotted signs for the lighted entrances to the main thoroughfare. He crossed under the bridge and then turned into the large business. He parked and opened his door and the scent of frying food tickled his gnawing stomach.

"Something smells good." His client had jumped from the SUV and moved next to him. She'd slung her backpack over one of her shoulders, reminding him they needed both food and light.

"Let's get inside and see how fast we can get something to eat." He limped forward, wishing he could offer her an arm and a smooth gait. Not having full use of both legs was irritating. Other after-effects had ruined his future, but he didn't want to think of those, especially when escorting an appealing woman. The fact that she held the door open for him to enter didn't do his ego any favors.

"It looks like they have a twenty-four-hour breakfast bar. I can smell the bacon from here and there might be a whiff of cinnamon roll calling my name." She followed him through the door, stepped around him, and led them toward the enticing aroma-filled cafe.

Sitting in a back corner hid them from the view of people in the store at the front of the business. They made quick work of devouring a hearty middle-of-the-night breakfast. The cinnamon rolls were huge, so they shared one. After their meal, Carlton patted his belly and sipped on an extra-large coffee while he watched Leah sift through the contents of her bag.

"Oh, no." She gasped and pulled out a small electronic device with a faint pulsing light. "Is this what you were wanting me to find?"

"Not really, but I'm glad you did."

"I guess they must have placed it in the bottom of my art supply bag when they wrecked my room. I just grabbed everything and stuffed it back in at the hotel. I didn't think about them putting anything in the bottom." Leah shuddered.

Carlton placed a finger to his lips and shook his head no as he spoke near the device. "There's probably nothing to worry about. Let's see what they have on the dessert menu."

Without saying another word, he took the tracker and tucked it under the seat cushion on his side of the booth. He dropped a tip on the table and grabbed the bill.

Leah brushed a lock of hair behind her ear as he nodded. He offered her a helping hand to climb from the booth. When her fingers contacted his hand, a flash of long-denied emotion spread across his heart. Why were his fingers tingling? He cleared his throat. They needed to hurry.

"Let's get going. They will track us to here if we don't leave soon."

"I have to make a pit stop." She looked nervously toward the restrooms.

"Good idea, but make it quick. Meet me right outside the bathroom doors. Check before you come all the way out to make sure I'm waiting for you." Carlton made record time paying the bill and using the men's facilities. Then he stood in the hallway listening. He heard the ladies' room hand-dryer turn on at the same time he heard a loud voice asking the store clerk if they'd seen a short, dark-haired woman and a man walking with a limp.

"Yeah. I think they went to the restaurant. You might check there." The clerk's answer was softer but understandable. He heard the hand-dryer turn off and then Leah peeped out. He placed a finger on his lips and pointed to the back exit. This time he did grab her elbow. Her support helped them make a rapid exit toward his SUV.

Once they'd belted themselves in, he started the vehicle and headed out of the parking lot. Looking in the rearview mirror he spotted the two men running for their sedan. Carlton turned east on a side road.

"I thought we were going to head for your office in Forest Glen." She twisted in her seat belt and looked behind them. "I think they spotted us."

"That's why we're headed in a different direction. I'll lose them at some point." At least that was what he hoped.

Chapter Five

Leah rubbed her eyes and stretched, waking from her half-doze. The SUV had stopped moving moments earlier and she'd been vaguely aware of Carlton opening his door and exiting the vehicle. She blinked and spotted the back of a building. Leah watched as Carlton looked around the area and then pulled a key from his pocket. Slipping out of the passenger door, she headed to his side. He waved her into the dark structure, then took her hand and led her forward until she heard a door close behind them. Carlton edged his way up a flight of stairs. She followed. At the top he opened another door. Lights flickered on, revealing a room with no windows, a desk with a matching chair, and a cot.

Carlton waved toward the cot with blankets folded at the end. "You can rest here in our emergency apartment. I'll catch a couple of winks at my desk and keep one ear open for trouble."

"I take it this must be Guardians Security Group's headquarters." Leah sat on the edge of the cot as he nodded.

"We're still a work in progress. One day the Guardians may grow big enough to have a bigger office and a fleet of business cars. For now we have this apartment above a small office. Kent started the business to install alarm systems and provide security at events. I doubt he planned on someone chasing and threatening us."

She wrapped a blanket around her shoulders. The warmth felt good. Her teeth chattered from either the cool room or the stressful night. "Did you have any more run-ins with our followers while I slept?"

"No. I left them in the dark." The ends of his lips turned up for the first time since she'd met him.

His grin made her heart do an unexpected flutter. He actually looked handsome when he wasn't frowning. She pulled the blanket tighter. "Thanks."

"Goodnight." Carlton turned off the lights and left the room.

Leah lay down on the cot and stared into the darkness. A dim light glowing from a land-line phone and a small clock on the desk served as nightlights once her eyes adjusted to the darkness. Sleep wasn't going to come easy. The nap in the SUV left her wide-awake and running scenarios through her mind about why the men so desperately wanted her latest rescue mule.

One thing was sure, they were not going to get Sylvester the mule again and inflict any more torture on the poor animal. Even if they discovered the location of her ranch, they wouldn't find him there. He'd developed an infection and at the moment, was safely hidden at her veterinarian's stables under a twenty-four-hour watch. Thinking of time, she reached over and turned the desk clock in her direction. It read 5:45. In another fifteen minutes her foreman, make that forewoman, Shannon, would start checking on the mules at the ranch. Leah needed to make her employee and friend aware of the situation.

Carlton had asked Leah to turn off her cell phone before she'd drifted off to sleep a few hours earlier in the SUV. He hadn't said anything about not using his company's landline sitting close by the cot. She sat up and watched the minutes tick away on the clock. Her thoughts started churning about maybe including Sylvester's back story into her comic strip. She'd never used her work for a political commentary before. Her characters had been humorous and fun. Maybe it was time to take a stand for the animals she loved. Right now, she needed to make sure they were safe.

She picked up the phone promptly at six and dialed Shannon's number, praying her employee would answer the call from an outside number. It rang several times before silence indicated someone had picked up and wasn't talking.

Leah's first reaction was panic, but then she remembered all the times they'd talked about whether to answer a call from an unknown number. Not many people had the ranch's number. Fewer had her reclusive forewoman's contact information, but there'd still been a few calls from scammers.

"Shannon, it's me. Leah."

"Hey, Boss. I wasn't sure who was calling. You're lucky I picked up."

"Not luck, I was praying you'd answer."

"You're right. So, what's got you calling this early? The time of day is the only thing that made me decide to answer. Did something happen with Sylvester at the vet's?"

The woman might be a loner, but she was as loyal to the mules as Leah. If the animals were under threat, Shannon would be the first to come to their defense.

Leah drew in a calming breath. She didn't need to upset Shannon any more than necessary, but the woman also needed the truth. "Not exactly. Our new rescue is fine as far as I know. I wanted to make you aware that someone is searching for Sylvester. Two crooks trying to find out his location accosted me at the comic convention."

Shannon gasped. "Are you all right?"

"I'm fine, but the bodyguard I hired had to do his job." Leah realized her comment came out a little snarky. Carlton had come through, even though she'd had her doubts.

"I'm glad he was there when you needed him. Why would anyone want Sylvester? He's not the healthiest or friendliest mule we've ever had at the rescue."

"They claim to be his former owners. We need to make sure those men don't get their hands on him again. Tell Paul and Josephine not to leak information about him, the location of the ranch, or the veterinarian's stable."

"I'll take care of everything here. Do you want me to contact Dr. Sanders?" Braying background noises filtered through the phone as Shannon made her offer.

"That would be great. Tell him to keep our boy safe. Also, contact the auction house that sold us Sylvester. See if they have any additional records of where he came from."

"I'll check, but the initial information they gave us only indicated they found Sylvester alone in a farmer's corn field."

A light from an opening door split the darkness.

"It won't hurt to ask again. I'm praying they don't have a legal tie to him." Leah couldn't keep her anger from her voice.

"What's going on here?" Carlton's demanding voice interrupted as he stepped into the apartment.

"Who's that?" Shannon asked.

"That would be my bodyguard, Carlton."

"That's my cue to leave." Leah heard a click as Shannon signed off.

"I needed to contact my ranch and make sure all is well." Leah slammed the phone down and pulled the blanket up to her neck.

"Next time, run any contact by me. When I woke from a nap, I heard you talking and noticed a phone line light. We don't know who might be watching or listening to what is said at this point in time."

"Understood." Leah rolled toward the wall. She closed her eyes and pretended to doze until sleep became real.

~~~~~

Carlton shook his head. That hadn't gone over well. He thumped his way down the stairs to the office. Now wasn't the time to continue his lecture on safety. He walked by a window and saw the sun peeping out in the eastern sky. Pinks, purples, and a hint of orange washed across the horizon. He watched for a few minutes longer until full light banished the multiple colors from view. He needed to make a call
~~~~~

himself and see what his boss, Kent Russell, wanted him to do.

"Hey, Kent. We're hiding out at headquarters. Mara is resting in the apartment. I'm checking in to see what our next step should be." Carlton slipped back to thinking of her as Mara.

Kent's scratchy voice answered. "I wondered who entered the building last night, but figured it might be you since the alarm was turned off with the correct code. Mara's agent tracked down my home phone number. She called a few minutes ago and didn't sound happy about losing contact with you two. She remembered my name but not the name of my business. Don't be surprised if she calls the office looking for you now that she knows who we are. She's worried about whether our client will make the next speaking engagement."

"Yeah, about that, I'm not sure going to another event is a good idea. These guys seem pretty serious and my, ah, leg hasn't been an advantage."

"Have some confidence in yourself. You've kept her safe to this point. Besides, Winnie Gee and her husband have secured the autograph table next to Mara's for this afternoon's book signing. My wife and I will be there for both of you, not that you need my help." Kent Russell chuckled at his inside joke.

Carlton knew Kent would take good care of his wife, an author and illustrator. Winnie Gee, formerly known as art teacher, Miss Freddie Grimsley, and now as Winnie Russell, had been a witness in their last mutual case as federal agents. After her testimony helped take down a ring of cybercriminals, Kent resigned from his government job and started Guardians Security Group.

During Winnie's case, a wild mule had barreled into Carlton, severely re-injuring a previous problem with his leg. Something kept clicking in the back of his mind. The dingy white mule with dark markings reminded him of Mara's Sylvester. He'd wondered about that earlier, but the bad guys had interrupted the conversation before he could finish asking her.

"Hey, Boss? Is there a reason you put me on this case? You know I'm still angry about my leg being ruined by a mule and this situation seems to be all about mules."

Carlton thought back. He'd never seen the woman who owned the wild mule. He hadn't wanted to meet her at the time. Kent had encouraged him to not explore the cause of his injuries and, to tell the truth, he hadn't really wanted to do anything but move on and try to salvage his life. He'd tried, though there were days when resentment overcame him with as much pain as his aching leg. Now he suspected that his boss had withheld important information.

After a long pause, Kent cleared his throat. "I thought getting to know Mara, also known as Leah Beach, would help you heal from the past. The time has come to forgive and move on. You need to let go of your resentment of mules, especially her Sylvester."

Carlton couldn't give Kent the answer he knew his boss wanted to hear. He sighed, wishing it were easy to say the words of forgiveness. "I'll see you at the book signing later today."

After hanging up, he put his face in his hands and leaned over the desk. He should forgive the mule and the owner, especially since it was Leah. The animal had only complicated his previous injury. His misfired weapon hadn't helped when the mule ran him over. Worse harm had happened before when criminals from a previous case shot his leg multiple times.

He'd nearly recovered from those wounds when his girlfriend left him. When he admitted the wounds resulted in lessening his chance to have children, Susie dropped him faster than a hot potato. He'd tried suggesting adoption, but that hadn't stopped her from walking away. Clenching his fists, he prayed.

Help me, Lord. I know I need to let this go and move on, but the pain makes it hard to forget.

He sat back and crossed his arms. It was difficult to forgive himself, much less someone else. Confidence in his abilities had taken another blow when a fellow agent had left a young girl in his care during the cybercriminal case. A kidnapper took the girl when Carlton was supposed to keep her safe.

Doubts about keeping Leah safe swirled across his mind. Hadn't she expressed concerns about his abilities and attitude earlier? She'd even helped with her own escape by jabbing her attackers with a pencil. At least Kent would be near them at today's event. After tonight, he'd ask his boss to transfer him to installing security systems. It might mean a demotion in pay, but he wasn't sure he deserved his present salary.

The office phone rang, drawing him out of his misery. "Guardians Security Group, how may I help you?"

"Where is my client, Mara Shore?" a now-familiar, strident voice demanded. She hurried on before Carlton could respond. "I woke up to the news she was no longer in the hotel. You should have notified me of the change immediately. Even your own boss wasn't sure where you were at. Leah should have shared this number or your personal one with me when she hired you. I need your assurance that she will attend the book signing today."

Carlton held the phone away as the literary agent blasted his ear with his shortcomings. Hearing his faults from her mouth made him want to defend his abilities. He sat a little straighter in the chair.

"I can assure you, ma'am, that your client is safe and will remain in our care until after the signing today. Have a wonderful day." Carlton put the phone back in the cradle and crossed his arms. Had Kent suggested the agent call the office or had she decided that on her own? He stifled a yawn. He just needed to keep himself together until Leah's contract ended at midnight.

Chapter Six

Leah woke with a start. She had a book signing today for her last stop on the tour, but her banner and other set-up items were most likely still at the hotel with her suitcase. Even though the clock indicated it was after nine in the morning, darkness shrouded the windowless room. If she could force herself to complete the tour, contacting Penny about retrieving the needed items for the signing was a priority. She sat up and managed to turn on the desk lamp. Sighing, she lifted the phone and dialed her agent's familiar number, using *67 before the numerals to hide her caller ID.

"Hey, Penny."

"It's about time you contacted me." Penny's grating voice rang in her ear like fingernails on a chalkboard. "Your bodyguard says you will be at the event today, but I need to hear it from your own lips."

"I will be there, but I left the banner and my suitcase in the hotel." Leah swallowed back her own angry words. Her agent had shown no mercy when it came to completing the tour.

"No need to worry about the banner and luggage. The hotel has already informed me of the need to pick up your things before checkout at noon. I'm heading there now. Do you at least have something decent to wear today?" Penny gave orders like a general.

"No." Leah had only gathered what was most important, her art materials.

Penny huffed. "Would you like to meet me where you're at right now or at the bookstore? You need to present a proper image."

Leah huffed. The less time she spent with Penny, the better. "Let's plan on meeting at the bookstore around 12:30. I'll change in their restroom and be ready before the signing starts."

"I guess that will have to do." The phone disconnected.

Leah stood and headed toward the door. She needed to find the facilities and make use of them. The downstairs office below her sleeping area revealed a woman sitting at a desk, concentrating on phone calls, and her bodyguard snoozing on a couch near a door labeled as a restroom.

Stepping into the small room she took care of her urgent needs and then stared into the mirror at the messy hair spiraling around her head. Ugh. Finger combing helped enough to tame her locks into a low ponytail secured with a tie from yesterday's braid. She'd need more care than that once Penny arrived at the signing venue. Her hairbrush and toiletries were in the suitcase left at the hotel. For now, having her hair pulled back from her face would have to do. Using paper towels and hand soap, she did her best to refresh her body before stepping back into the office.

"Good morning, Miss Shore." Carlton stretched as he came to a sitting position. A few strands of hair stood awry from his nap. Without having his face wrinkled up in worry, he looked younger and more handsome than he'd been the day before.

Leah wondered what it would be like to settle his mussed curls back into place. She stuffed her hands in her pockets to keep from acting on her thoughts. Instead, she decided to remind him he had permission to use her first name since he'd just addressed her by her pen name. "Remember, unless we're in public, please feel free to call me Leah."

A flicker of a smile crossed his face. "I can do that, at least when we're not around your agent. She's already called Kent and me this morning to make sure you're at the signing today." His smile turned into a frown. "Is she always so unpleasant?"

"Penny was fine when I hired her. Now she mostly centers her thoughts on making money. I'm sorry if she gave you a rough time." Leah looked directly into his eyes.

He shook his head and looked down. "I'm the one who should be apologizing. I'm sorry I didn't take guarding you seriously at first. I wish I didn't have this limp. Kent should have given you a healthy bodyguard."

"You did well, in spite of your leg. We made it here in one piece. Now you just have to get me through today. Then you can be off to another security detail." Leah meant what she said. His driving skills and defensive use of the cane were impressive.

"We'll have extra help today. My boss will be at the signing with his wife, author Winnie Gee." His shoulders sank. His expression still seemed apologetic.

"Wonderful. We've met before. That's the reason I called the Guardians." Leah clapped her hands. She looked forward to talking with the couple again.

"When did you meet Winnie?" Carlton smoothed down his hair and leaned forward, once more drawing Leah's attention to his good looks.

She swallowed before answering. "Actually, it was Sylvester who introduced me to Kent. Mr. Russell was working as a federal agent back when Sylvester first came to my rescue ranch."

Leah watched color fade from Carlton's face as his mouth gaped open. "Kent mentioned something about that earlier. You just reminded me of my worst nightmare. Your mule..." He clamped his hands into fists and leaned forward. A wrinkle crossed his brow.

"Are you okay?" Leah asked.

~~~~~

No. Carlton was not okay. He'd finally started to heal from an assailant's gunshot to his leg when her uncontrollable mule barreled into him, causing his gun to go off, reinjuring and causing irreparable damage to his leg. Due to time in the hospital, he'd never had contact with the mule's owner. Resentment had built. Depression held him in its grip until Kent offered to hire Carlton at his new company, the Guardians Security Group.

He'd accepted the invitation, knowing he had to move on and find a way to make a living. Despite the new job, he still harbored resentment over the run-in with the mule. He often made his thoughts about the incident clear to those around him.

Kent suggested forgiveness was part of the healing process. Carlton knew his boss was right, but hadn't managed to offer forgiveness, not that anyone asked for his pardon. If Leah didn't know about the harm her mule did, Kent must not have informed her about the damage incurred. How did Carlton handle that? Kent might be his boss, but right now the man had some explaining to do about assigning Carlton to Leah as a bodyguard.

"Carlton? Did you hear me? Are you okay?" Leah waved a hand in front of his face.

"I'm fine." He spoke with his teeth clenched. He was anything but fine and he knew it. He needed to get a grip and have some space to think through things. He stood and paced around the room.

She padded along right behind him on his second lap and laid a hand on his forearm. "I'm sorry if I upset you." Her voice shook.

"No worries. I just have a couple of issues I need to work through with the boss." He turned and looked at her when she withdrew her hand and wrapped her arms around her shaking body.

"What did Kent tell you about your mule during the federal operation?" His voice came out harsher than he meant it to.

"Just that Sylvester needed to stay on his own property while the federals were set up on my neighbor's ranch. I didn't know that neighbor and I still don't. I've avoided them and didn't make further contact after that event was over. My mule got away twice during the federal operation. That's all I know, other than I met Winnie Gee and Kent's grandkids when I went there to collect Sylvester the first time he ran away."
~~~~~

"Did he inform you about the next time your mule got away?" Carlton studied her face for any clue that she knew what had happened between him and her runaway animal.

"Kent brought Sylvester back the second time he got away. Sylvester was gone for over a week. I assumed he was somewhere on my property and looked for him there, until Kent showed up. I offered another apology for Sylvester trespassing. After that, we kept in contact and I got to know Winnie, or Freddie as he often calls her. He's one of the few people who know where my ranch is located. I asked him to keep that information and my author identity to himself. The only other person who knows is Winnie. He doesn't keep secrets from his wife."

Carlton wanted to growl or throw something but figured from Leah's wide eyes and how she took a step away from him that she was already scared of what he might do. Instead, he scribbled nonsense on a notepad, wadded the paper up, and then tossed it into the trash.

Kent had obviously kept it a secret from his former federal agent and employee. It seemed his boss had also kept Leah in the dark about her mule harming Carlton. Or maybe he'd missed a few of Kent's subtle hints about not holding grudges against people owning mules. Carlton hadn't been happy about her mule cartoons when Kent assigned him to Mara's, make that Leah's, protection duty.

He drew a calming breath. "Did Kent ever say anything about what the mule had done when he brought Sylvester back to you?"

She shook her head. "He just returned him. I think Kent was a little star-struck when he saw some of my artwork in the barn office. Then he started talking about how he was going to marry Winnie Gee and suggested the three of us ought to get together sometime."

"I've never heard him mention meeting you before." Carlton tapped the pencil he'd been scribbling with on the pad of paper. The lead broke.

"I made the choice for them. I'm not too social, so we've ended up only meeting online from time to time and kept it quiet. They're some of my only acquaintances outside of my ranch workers and my agent. Though, Penny doesn't even know where the ranch is located. Something inside keeps me from sharing that location with her."

"Your ranch might be a good place to hang out after the book signing today." Carlton grimaced. "I think hiding from Penny is a good idea. She isn't a pleasant person. Maybe you need to get a new agent."

"I've thought about it, but it's hard for me to get to know new people. I'm hoping she'll be happy with the sales this tour is producing and will be more content once those royalties arrive."

"How long does it take for the money to come in?" Carlton was glad the conversation had drifted to something other than Kent's omissions concerning what the mule had done.

"The publishers send royalties out four times a year. We're both hoping for a good profit from the graphic novel. I'll be grateful because the rescue ranch recently lost a major supporter and Penny must have something she wants to spend her money on."

"Couldn't you ask your dad to support your ranch? I'm sure he has plenty of funds from all his work as a well-known cartoonist with television and movie credits."

Leah turned away and headed for the stairs leading to the apartment where he'd left her sleeping last night. "I need to get my things together. Is there a place where I can get a shower before we leave for the signing?"

Her words came out muffled as she hurried away. He wondered if she might be crying but couldn't be sure. One thing was certain. She didn't want to talk about her father. He guessed they both had things bothering them and that was fine at the moment. He needed time to think and had some questions for Kent to answer.

After she closed the apartment door, he called Kent's home number.

"What were you thinking when you asked me to take this case? The more I think about it, the more I wish I didn't have to deal with this. You know I still have issues with my recovery. Her mule being involved makes this personal." Carlton knew his words were harsh, but couldn't help feeling betrayed by Kent's lack of transparency regarding the mule incident.

"I am aware of your resentment, but I also know it's time for you to get over yourself and move on. Forgiveness will help. Dwelling on the past won't change your physical limitations. Neither will piling guilt on Leah's shoulders. I've been praying you'd get to know her and realize you could forgive what happened. She had no control over the damage her mule or your gun did to you."

Carlton paused before answering. Kent had played him, but his boss meant well. "I'll think about it." He shook his head. "In the meantime, we need a place where Leah can get cleaned up. Can we stop by your house for a few minutes before the book signing today?"

"No problem. Bring her over now and we'll have time to visit. Winnie will be excited to see her."

Carlton hung up without acknowledging the invitation or bidding Kent goodbye. He stared at the closed door, wondering how long it took for a person without a change of clothes to get ready.

Fifteen minutes later, she emerged with her backpack slung over her shoulders and headed over to stand by the front door. Her head bent forward as she focused on the floor in front of her.

He cleared his throat and pointed to the rear door once she looked up. "My SUV is out back. Kent's house isn't far from here. You can take your shower there."

Her only answer was a quick nod before she trudged toward the exit.

"Wait." Carlton hobbled to the door. "I need to make sure we don't have any trouble before we go out."

Her eyes widened briefly. She hugged herself and leaned against the wall next to the door.

"I'll be out back for a minute. Stay in here with our other bodyguard, Cara, until I come back in." After she nodded, he stepped outside and circled around his vehicle. Everything looked in order except for a handprint smeared near his rear bumper. He snapped a picture and then took a knee next to where it appeared someone had done the same. Bending his head to the side, he looked beneath the end of his car and spotted what appeared to be a magnetized tracking device making its presence known by periodic flashes of green light.

Chapter Seven

Leah watched Carlton push off the ground and awkwardly rise to his feet. He stared at something in his hand, before heading back toward the building.

She stepped aside to let him in. "What did you find?"

He opened his palm. "It looks like they found us last night and decided to leave another tracker instead of interrupting your rest." He placed the electronic device on a shelf near the door. "We'll leave this here for now. Maybe they'll think we're still resting."

"I wonder why they didn't come inside to get us." Relief and worry warred inside her thoughts. While she was glad for the rest and lack of conflict, the presence of the gadget was upsetting.

"Since they seem to want the mule more than they want you, I'm going to guess they hoped we'd take off for the ranch this morning."

"I'm glad we didn't head there. Are we safe going to Kent and Winnie's home?" Wariness washed over her as she thought about drawing her acquaintances into her troubles.

Carlton interrupted her concerns. "We'll head there now. The Russells are anxious to have you visit their place, since you've only met online."

"Yeah." She didn't feel like going into details about her solitary lifestyle. After the book signing, the relationship with Guardians Security would be over unless she decided to extend their contract. She shivered. Retaining their services looked like a strong possibility now.

"Then let's get on our way before the mule people change their minds about following us. The Russells' home isn't too far outside of Forest Glen." Carlton motioned her toward the truck and held the door open.

She trudged forward and climbed into the seat, wishing she was home at her ranch working with the needy mules. She'd rescued many of them over the last few years. None of their former owners had given her trouble before. Most were relieved to give up an animal that was as stubborn as they were. Mules were loyal to those who gave them the time and attention they deserved. Many former owners were as much at fault as their long-eared steeds.

Sylvester had plenty of faults when it came to accepting new people. She could identify with that problem. Clearly, both she and her newest mule had trust issues. She'd been hurt by her only boyfriend, who kidnapped her after learning about her rich father. That event soured her relationship with her father and most people.

What had those men done to betray Sylvester? Did his current infection have any underlying cause from their abuse? The veterinarian mentioned the possibility of removing something abnormal buried deep under Sylvester's skin. She'd given permission for the operation, but the doctor was waiting for doses of antibiotics to clear up the infection before cutting into Sylvester's shoulder.

"You're awfully quiet over there. Is there anything you'd like to share?" Carlton's voice interrupted her thoughts.

She shook her head and then thought it might be a good idea to share. "Sylvester has something lodged deep in one of his shoulders. He's at the vet's barn right now getting heavy-duty antibiotics so the doctor can get rid of the infection before operating. I wonder if that has anything to do with the abuse he suffered before he came to my ranch."

Leah watched as Carlton rounded a corner and turned left into the driveway of a modest split-level home. "We'll run that by Kent. Let's get inside and see what he thinks." He put the car in park as he looked one way and then the other. The garage door creaked open. He waved to the couple standing inside. "Let's move."

Leah didn't wait. She ran into the open portal and hugged the older woman who sported a messy bun.

Winnie wrapped her arms around Leah surrounding her with comfort. "Welcome, little magpie. We're glad you came to see us in person." The older woman's words and physical expression of endearment warmed Leah. She hadn't had that kind of welcome in years.

"I'm so glad to be here. I just wish it was under different circumstances." Leah looked down as shame about bringing trouble to others made her chest tighten.

Winnie shifted to Leah's side and linked elbows as they stepped into the house. The smell of something roasting in the oven made Leah's stomach rumble. They hadn't eaten since the diner's overnight breakfast. She hoped her hostess hadn't heard the protest from her belly.

"Don't you worry about a thing. My Kent and his agent Carlton will keep you from harm. They did their best to keep me safe when I had my own troubles. I'm here today, thanks to their efforts, and ready to sign some books this afternoon. How about you?" Winnie led her to a couch, and they sat down together.

"I'm ready for this tour to be over. Signing those books will make me one step closer to being home with my mules. Going cross-country with my graphic novel hasn't been my favorite thing to do."

Winnie gave Leah's hand a pat. "Isn't this your first tour?"

"Yes. I wish it could be my last." Leah looked down as the other woman squeezed her hand.

"My first presentation was scary, but then I learned to enjoy my readers. I'm sure there have been some positive moments." Winnie smiled as she made eye contact.

Leah closed her eyes and thought back to the children she'd met the day before and along the way. "There have. I met many families who were delightful."

"Then those contacts made it worth your time. Someone told me that if my books touched one life then the work to write and share the book was worth the effort. If nothing else, Kent's grandsons have proven my stories reached at least a couple of hearts." Winnie smiled at her husband.

"You mean our grandsons, sweetheart." Kent grinned back with obvious affection.

"Yes, I do." She waved her husband to the empty seat on the couch. "We're newlyweds and I'm still getting used to my new family. I'm enjoying being a parent and grandmother." She turned back to Leah. "Are your parents worried about you and your mules?"

"I haven't shared anything with Dad. Mom is no longer with us. He and I aren't close. If you'll excuse me, I really do need to get cleaned up." Leah looked away and gazed at the paintings decorating their walls. She needed a distraction.

"Sure, hon. I laid out towels and some clean clothes for your use. They're probably a little big, but they should do until your suitcase catches up to you. Kent explained that your agent is bringing your suitcase to the bookstore. Our restroom is the first door on the right."

"Thanks."

Leah closed herself in the bathroom and sank down on the toilet seat. Telling her dad wouldn't do them any good. That bridge had burned years ago, and she wasn't ready to rebuild it.

~~~~~

With his arms crossed, Carlton plopped down into an easy chair located beneath a mask from some overseas culture and waited for his boss to say something. At the same time, he hoped Kent wouldn't lecture him on forgiveness. He was still working through his issues with Leah's mule.

Kent sat opposite him on the couch with Winnie. The man raised an eyebrow but kept silent when his wife patted his knee.

Winnie leaned forward as she wagged her pointer in the air. "Aren't you a little old to have a pity party? You sound like one of my former
~~~~~

students who had a blob of paint ruin his work. The past is over and there's not much you can do about it other than stand up to your problems and overcome them. Make something interesting out of that blot that stands in your way. Trust me, I learned the hard way that it is better to solve problems than run away from them. I lived a lonely life until I found the Lord's forgiveness and Kent's. Now I'm transforming that stain on the past into a wonderful future."

"Leah hasn't asked for forgiveness." Carlton knew he whined like the child Winnie had compared him to. Her lecture made him squirm like a visit to the principal's office. The quiet pause in the conversation was also uncomfortable when Winnie didn't respond to his comment.

Kent broke his silence. "That's because Leah didn't know all the details. I hadn't planned to be the one to tell her, since it might have been the mule or perhaps it was your gun that misfired and damaged your leg."

"Maybe you need to forgive yourself for being resentful. God can help you with that too." Winnie's gentle voice whispered hope and reason into his mind.

They were right, but it was hard to move on when reminders of the event came with each step he took on his weakened leg. He'd blamed the mule for everything, but his gun had played a role. One he hadn't planned. Carlton shuddered as his shoulders slumped forward. Admitting he'd been part of the injury was hard. He closed his eyes and prayed for strength to do his job for the rest of the day. Then he could move on and never have a need to see or hear about another mule. Warm hands rested on his shoulders. Kent and Winnie added their prayers to his. He reached up and placed his hands over theirs as peace washed his soul clean.

Carlton acknowledged his uphill battle.

"Thank you. I'll try to do my best to get over myself. This is something I will need to keep working on."

"Good. Now bring me up to speed on what has been going on." Kent transformed into boss mode as Winnie excused herself to check on lunch.

Carlton detailed the threats to Leah and the mule, Sylvester.

Kent laughed. "She kept the silly name one of my agents gave the mule. Victor said there was a children's book about a mule or donkey with that name. I guess the moniker stuck."

"Leah also said she's been keeping the exact location of her ranch a secret from her agent and the outside world. I'm not a fan of the agent myself, so I can understand not sharing. It might be a good idea to do a background check on Penny Barrington since she seems overly concerned about making money from our client's writing."

"I'll have someone look into her. It wouldn't surprise me if she's just trying to make more money. Agents have to make a living, too, according to my Winnie."

Carlton cleared his throat. "I didn't mention it to Leah, but I realize her ranch must be near Tamera's place. She mentioned a reclusive neighbor when I was recovering at her home the first time around." And also the second time, but Carlton didn't want to bring up his injury again.

Kent's voice broke into his thoughts. "She asked Winnie and me to keep her secret too. She mentioned a strained family relationship and enduring a teen kidnapping as reasons for the secrecy. Do we need to set up security at Leah's place?"

"For the time being, I think putting someone at the mule's veterinarian might be our next move. Sylvester has an infection. Once he is in better shape the vet will operate on something in one of his shoulders. It might be an implant. Leah and I wondered if that could be related to the threats."

Kent pulled his ever-present notepad and pen from his shirt pocket and started jotting down notes. "We'll look into that possibility. So many horses and mules that have lived out their usefulness end up sold off to the proverbial glue factory. An unscrupulous lab could have bought the mule for an experiment, and they need their implant back. Or, the implant only indicates ownership, and they don't want us to find out who they are."

Carlton waited for his boss to finish writing. The smell of roasted meat drew a hungry growl from his stomach. The sound of an oven door opening, followed by the clatter of a pan lid made his mouth water.

Kent rubbed his belly. "It sounds like our meal is ready as soon as our guest is done showering."

"Do we need to set the table?" Carlton rose to help.

"Winnie put out her best china before she started cooking. I married a very capable woman." Kent's satisfied expression was obvious. If Carlton guessed correctly, he'd say his boss had gained a few pounds since being married.

The doorway to the bathroom opened and the aroma of lavender-scented soap emerged, along with his refreshed client. Carlton swallowed as he took in the view. She was gorgeous. His heart pounded in his chest.

Kent bumped Carlton's shoulder. "I take it you don't want me to get another operative to watch over our client, even if this takes a few days."

"Nope."

Chapter Eight

Leah's eyes met Carlton's as she slipped from the bathroom. She touched her damp hair, wondering if something was out of place as she watched Kent bump her grinning bodyguard. Men. Or should she say *boys*? Stashing her stack of dirty laundry in the hallway, she headed toward the sound of Winnie humming in the kitchen.

"Thanks for the use of your bath and extra clothing." She watched Winnie lift a beef roast from a deep baking pan.

"No problem, sweet magpie. I've had my share of adventures in the past. As you well remember, Kent had to rescue me from my own set of bad guys. Now I have my own handsome protector." Winnie raised her eyebrows.

Ugh. Too much, too soon. "I appreciate Carlton's help. I hope he can keep me safe today and then we can all be off to different paths. May I help you?"

"Sure. Take the meat to the table while I put the carrots and potatoes in bowls." Winnie smiled as she lifted the plate toward her willing helper. "You probably noticed that our Carlton is a handsome man. Don't let that walking cane get in the way of a friendship, or more."

Leah rolled her eyes. "I appreciate your thoughts, but I have no plans to get involved with anyone. My mule rescue and comics occupy all my time. I just can't understand why anyone would want to harm an animal." She took the dish to the dining room where the two men stood eyeing the set table. Their gaze followed what she held in her hand, while they sniffed at a preset platter of rolls. At least Carlton wasn't focusing on her. She took a deep breath and placed the warm plate on a quilted table runner.

Winnie entered with the other two dishes and set them near the meat. "Let's eat and then we can head out to our book signing." She stayed standing until Kent pulled out her chair.

Leah slid into her chair when Carlton turned her way. After Winnie's comment and the men gawking at her earlier, she didn't need any gallantry. She bowed her head and listened to Kent's prayer.

"Dear Heavenly Father, thank You for the bounty we are about to receive. Help us use the strength we gain for Your good. Bless our guest and keep her safe from those who would seek to harm her. Guide Carlton and me as we guard our ladies today. In Jesus' Name we pray,

Amen."

Staring at the food, Leah added her own unspoken prayer for safety from the enemy threatening her mule, and the matchmaking couple.

"Potatoes?" Carlton held the bowl out to her. His face was as red as she imagined her own was. His lips formed the silent word "sorry" as he released the serving dish to her hands.

"Thanks. I could use some starch right now." She straightened in her seat and looked at the older couple. "No offense, but I think we should be concentrating on protection for my mule and me, rather than anything else."

Kent had the decency to duck his head. "My apologies."

Winnie nodded in agreement and reached out to give Leah's arm a gentle squeeze.

Carlton cleared his throat. "Kent shared the layout for the book signing with me earlier. We'll be along the back wall of the bookstore. There are two other authors. Winnie knows both of them. We'll be standing by your center tables with the other authors on each side."

Kent's fork clunked as he set it down. "I also asked Cara, my other security employee, to roam around the front of the store. You might have met her earlier this morning at the office. The business knows she will be there, so they won't question her presence. I've made her aware there are two men working together."

"Butter anyone?" Winnie lifted the dish and frowned at her husband. "I didn't fix this meal for you to turn it into a planning session. Let's fill our tummies with the food you just blessed."

"Here's to the cook." Kent lifted his water glass and took a sip.

Leah lifted a fork full of carrots in salute as she tried to dismiss her concerns for the afternoon. The delicious vegetable melted in her mouth, adding physical strength she'd need for the author visit at the mall bookstore.

~~~~~

An hour later she sat in Carlton's vehicle as they followed Kent and Winnie to the event. Carlton was silent. She couldn't think of anything to say either. Relief that no one had hinted about relationships for the rest of the meal made her glad for the silence they maintained until reaching the strip mall where the bookstore anchored one end.

Carlton cleared his throat. "There's something that's been bothering me. I need to talk to you about it." He sounded serious.

"What's the matter?"

"I need to clear the air about something that happened to me, since Kent and Winnie haven't had the courage to come clean about what happened during the federal sting related to Winnie's case."
~~~~~

Her heart sank. She doubted the older couple would withhold the truth from her. "What are you talking about?"

"When Sylvester ran away the second time, he and I tangled with each other, causing my weapon to go off. I ended up in the hospital. It wasn't pretty. I've been angry about the re-injury he helped cause during our run in. After talking to Kent this morning, I realize the need to forgive him and try to get over any resentment that has been in my thoughts."

"How can you be sure it was Sylvester?"

"I wasn't sure at first. He was covered in mud and I didn't clearly see any of his spots. Kent revealed the truth when I recently questioned him. He knew I was having problems with my anger concerning the situation that changed my life."

"I'm sorry." Leah couldn't think of anything else to say. Her mind was numb from the revelation. She stared out the window until they approached the bookstore for the autograph session.

Penny stood by her car with arms crossed. She looked at her watch as they pulled into a nearby parking spot. "It's about time you showed up." The agent leaned into her car and pulled out Leah's suitcase and hangers with a freshly pressed Western outfit. The rhinestone-covered blouse was one Leah had never seen before. Ironing the wrinkles out of a pair of jeans was unheard of on a mule rescue ranch.

"You picked out my clothes and ironed my jeans?" For some reason Leah felt violated. The woman might be her agent, but going through her clothing for the pants and buying something new went beyond expectations in an uncomfortable way. She bit her tongue to keep from saying something else. Between Carlton's revelation about Sylvester, the recent threats, and her pushy agent, her patience was almost gone.

"You need to dress your best when you do these appearances." Penny looked Leah up and down. "You're not exactly wearing clothing right now to sell books about mules. You're dressed like a grandma, if you want my opinion. Your audience is much younger. I'm counting on you to make us both wealthy, Miss Mara Shore." She shoved the clothing and suitcase into Leah's hands.

Leah took the items and marched toward the store ahead of her agent and her bodyguard. She needed to find a one-person restroom and get away from her agent, before she did something she'd regret. At the moment, her agent might need a bodyguard more than Leah. Firing the woman was no longer questionable. She needed to do it sooner rather than later.

~~~~~

Carlton followed Leah into the bookstore and stood guard outside
~~~~~

the restroom. When Leah, make that Mara, asked the manager for access to the employee facilities, the worker had smiled and led the famous author to the private room.

Penny had huffed when Leah closed the door in her face. "Tell Mara I'll be setting up the banner for her table. I hope you can do your job today and keep her safe." She looked down at his cane before marching away on clicking high heels.

Carlton shook his head. A flicker of doubt crossed his mind and then he lifted his chin. His cane might slow him down, but his actions over the last day had proven the device also worked as an effective weapon. Besides, he didn't need another sermon on pity parties from Winnie. Between her advice, Kent's encouragement, and their prayers, he'd do the best he could.

"Is she gone?" Leah peeked around the restroom door.

"Yeah. She said she'd set up the Mara Shore banner for the autographing session." Carlton watched in admiration as Leah stepped out wearing the well-fitting outfit the agent had chosen.

"That should keep her busy for a while. She has a tendency toward perfectionism. Ironed jeans are evidence of that trait, and I've never worn a shirt with rhinestones." Leah ran a hand down her side, looking unsure of her appearance.

He focused his gaze on her face, praying the warmth under his collar wasn't climbing into his cheeks. "I guess she thinks all the sparkle and shine will make people buy more books. Besides, you looked fine yesterday."

Pink washed across her face. He hadn't meant to embarrass his client. Making her uncomfortable wasn't a smart move, and he didn't want her to get the wrong idea. Carlton still felt the sting of rejection from his former fiancée. Looking away, he led her toward the author area where Kent spread a cloth over his wife's table.

Penny Barrington and Winnie stood behind the neighboring area holding the banner advertising Mara's book. "Don't move, Winnie. I'm going to clip my end to the edge of this shelf and then come over to do your side."

Carlton knew the minute Penny laid eyes on him. She pointed his way. "Get over here and make yourself useful by holding this end so it doesn't slip out of place. I need to make sure this banner is straight, and it's hard to see from here."

Carlton scowled at the woman before taking his place at the far end of the hanging. Penny moved back and held up her pointer fingers in a right angle.

"Raise your end by half an inch, Winnie. Good." The agent rushed over and clipped the other end of the banner. "Thanks, sweetie. Now, have you given any consideration to my offer? I'd be more than honored to represent Winnie Gee books."

Carlton couldn't believe the woman's nerve. He looked at Leah, who rolled her eyes.

Winnie laid a hand on the pushy woman's arm. "I've never worked with an agent. Since I've only had one publishing company during my entire career, there really isn't a need. The publisher, editor, and I have always worked well together."

"I'm sure I could negotiate a better contract and get you some work from other publishers." Penny leaned closer and slid her arm through the older woman's elbow.

"Like I told you before, I'm happy with my situation and don't need other work. Being a grandmother and wife takes up the rest of my time." Winnie wiggled out of the agent's grasp and took Kent's hand. "Being a newlywed takes up a fair amount of devotion too."

"Is there a reason for wanting more work of your own, Miss Barrington?" Carlton interrupted the exchange. He'd had enough of the woman badgering both his client and his boss's wife about making more money and decided on a direct approach. Maybe if the woman explained herself, they'd save energy on investigating her financial situation.

Penny squinted at Carlton. Her tight lips twisted to one side before she jutted out her chin. "An agent's job is to get the most money she can for her clients."

"And for yourself?" Carlton watched her body language. He suspected Penny wasn't comfortable answering his questions.

"That's how an agent makes a living." She spun away, pulled a couple of plastic frames from a bag, and placed them on the table. One held a picture and nameplate for Mara Shore, author and illustrator. The other held a reproduction of the graphic novel cover and clippings from the mule comic strip.

Penny put her hands on her hips. "I've gone above and beyond my normal duties to go with her on this book tour. I hope you two can perform up to my expectations. Now it's time for Mara to do her job by autographing plenty of books. Just do your assignment and guard her today without messing up."

"I assure you that won't be a problem. If for some reason I fail, I have backup this time from my boss, Kent." Carlton watched Penny's complexion fade.

"Excuse me. I think we're all set up now and I need to take a break." Penny tapped numbers into her phone as she walked to the front of the store. One hand mussed her perfectly styled hair as she stared out the window, talking.

"What was that all about?" Leah's breath whispered against the side of his arm, sending a shiver of awareness through his frame.

He stepped away and turned to face her. "Earlier, you mentioned her desire for making more money. I decided to ask a direct question. Her reaction may be nothing, but it's making me suspicious. Did you notice anything unusual in her answers?"

"From her actions just now, I'd say she doesn't like you very much." Leah's lips twitched as she took her place behind the author table.

Carlton nodded and took a seat as Leah continued.

"She's been a good agent until recently. Things seem different now. Penny is more money-driven and concerned about things being perfect than she was when I first contracted with her. She's even put more pressure on me about visiting the rescue ranch, which is odd. She's never had a personal interest in mules or even horses."

"Do you have an idea about when she may have started changing? Do you think it has anything to do with Sylvester the mule?" Carlton asked.

"I don't think so. She started getting cross at least six months back. Sylvester wasn't in the comics until a few weeks ago." Leah picked up a pen and tapped it on a stack of sticky notes.

Winnie waved from her table and lifted her marker as Kent rose to stand behind his wife. "Hey, you two, here come some fans. Get ready to autograph, Miss Mara Shore."

Carlton stood behind Leah and searched the crowd. Penny stood near a table of Leah's books, pointing to the volumes. She smiled at the Guardians' undercover woman, Cara, who appeared to be browsing for something to read. Maybe suspecting the agent was wrong. Penny seemed actively engaged in making the book signing a success, but something still felt off.

Chapter Nine

Three hours later, Leah autographed her last book for the day. The line of excited fans had dwindled during the final twenty minutes, giving her time to shake her cramping hand between visiting with readers.

"Here you go, Sandy, enjoy your book."

"Thank you, Miss Shore. Will Sylvester be in your next graphic novel?" The youngster beamed at the author and illustrator.

"I'm working on one right now and Sylvester will have a role." After today's event ended, she'd have even more time to devote to the sequel that readers and her agent begged for.

"Yay." The girl hugged her book and waved as she backed away, bumping into her mother.

Winnie grinned from the next table. "You have some great fans."

"I enjoy meeting them. They're older than your readers for the most part." Leah leaned back in her chair and released a deep sigh.

"Picture books have two readers, the child and the adult. In a few years my munchkins will be lined up at your table instead of mine." Winnie held up her latest book as she turned toward Leah. "Would you..."

Leah's phone buzzed in her pocket, interrupting the conversation. She recognized the number of Shannon, her forewoman at the rescue ranch. Holding up a finger, she mouthed that she needed to answer and then walked away from the autograph tables. "Hey, Shannon, what's up?"

"I did some more digging into Sylvester's background. The auction house asked the farmer who found him to give me a call. He confirmed what we already knew, but did mention he first sighted Sylvester on the north end of his property. By the time someone responded, the mule had moved to a cultivated field on the southern part of his farm. He called the Humane Society. They don't normally deal with mules, so they turned him over to the auction house. I guess they figured Sylvester was nearly dead and ready for the proverbial glue factory, especially with his ornery attitude." The sound of braying echoed through the connection. Shannon must have called from the barn.

Curiosity coursed through Leah. "Where's the farm located?"

"The place is several miles outside the town limits of Forest Glen, in a rural area across the road from a line of factories and other large buildings."

"Please text the address to me. I'd like to check it out." The sooner Leah figured out Sylvester's mystery, the better. She didn't care for being out in public, and so far the two men threatening her had found her in the city. Visiting a farm would be a breath of fresh air. Though having factories nearby wasn't appealing. She walked back toward where Penny and Carlton dismantled her author table as she listened to Shannon.

"Make sure you take someone with you. Bob Walton, the farmer I talked with, seemed like a nice guy, but snooping around those factories might not be safe." Shannon reminded Leah of a mother hen.

Without thinking she blurted, "That's why I'm paying for a bodyguard." She would start with the farm. Going into the factory area held no appeal, but she'd consider checking out the exteriors of the buildings if it would end the harassment of Sylvester and herself. Once she had the business names, then research online would be something she could do.

Carlton and Penny both stopped taking down the Mara Shore banner and stared at Leah. She shrugged and turned away to wrap up her telephone conversation. When she rotated back, her agent and bodyguard were still looking at her.

"I take it you want to continue our contract beyond today's event?" Carlton's expression showed mixed emotions.

"By the look on your face, I take it that you're not exactly thrilled to keep working for me." Leah fisted her hands as she searched Carlton's face.

"Sorry, you caught me off-guard. Our agency is more than happy to keep you safe until we can put an end to the threats to you and your mule. I've seen what your enemies are capable of doing."

Penny stepped next to Leah. "I'd be happy to be in charge of your safety. You don't need to waste your money on a half-there bodyguard." A closed-lip smile spread across Penny's face, not quite reaching her eyes. She took the banner from Carlton's hands and continued folding it.

Kent stepped next to Carlton. "My employee has done an excellent job. I would not have assigned Carlton to this case if I felt otherwise. Miss Shore needs a professional, not a helpful acquaintance."

Carlton stood straighter. "Miss Shore has the final say. I'm ready to serve her to the best of my ability."

Leah nodded. "Good. I want Carlton to continue working for me." She turned to Penny. "We need to discuss the terms of our future professional relationship."

Penny pasted a weak smile on her pale face. "Please forgive me. I've been under pressure lately with some personal issues. I value our relationship." She started picking up pens and bookmarks from the table. "Let's get you packed up so you'll be ready for a future tour."

Leah crossed her arms. "About any future books..."

Penny choked up as she sandwiched one of Leah's hands between hers. "I'm so sorry for my attitude in the last few months. I've let my personal life interfere with our business. You are my best talent and I love being your agent. Having someone like you as a client is more than I could ask for as an agent. I have great plans for promoting your next book." Tears appeared on her cheeks.

Leah sighed. Penny almost sounded like the woman she'd hired a year ago. Giving her another chance would set a Christian example. Choosing caution, Leah paused before answering. She needed to clear the air. "For our relationship to work, I need your support. Working under your pressure and criticism hasn't been ideal. If you are willing to make adjustments, I will weigh that in my final decision. You have two weeks."

"I'll do my best." Penny placed the last of the author paraphernalia into a box and smoothed down her outfit. A confident expression once again crossed her face. She smiled and then her lips tightened. "Could we meet for lunch tomorrow? I'd like to take you to a special restaurant as thanks for giving me an opportunity to redeem myself."

"I think that could be arranged. If I haven't resolved the issue with my new mule, you can expect my bodyguard to be in attendance." Leah watched Penny's shoulders tighten and then release.

"That will be fine." The agent lifted the box into her arms. "Would you like these in Carlton's vehicle?"

"Sure." Leah retrieved her suitcase and headed for the parking lot.

"That was an interesting exchange." Carlton walked next to Leah. "May I carry your bag?"

She shook her head. "I can handle my suitcase. I just hope I made the right decision regarding Penny."

~~~~~

Carlton put the GPS coordinates into his phone for the farm where Leah wanted to go. Kent and Winnie had evening plans with their foster granddaughter's family, Scott and Ginny Hallmark, but had offered Leah a place to stay for the night. After the older couple left, Carlton was once again on solitary protection duty. He hoped they weren't heading into more trouble, but Leah assured him she only wanted to talk to the man who'd found Sylvester. She'd contacted the farmer, Bob Walton, on her cell and asked if they could stop by to see where Sylvester had
~~~~~

roamed.

Before they drove ten miles, his passenger was asleep. Delicate eyelashes rested on her tanned cheeks. Crossed arms shielded her body. At least she trusted him to drive during the forty-five-minute trip. Frequent mirror checks proved no one followed. He was surprised not to see a sign of the agent. Penny had put on a big repentance plea, but he wasn't convinced she'd make any changes. Leah had given her one more chance than he would have. Carlton ran a hand down the side of his aching leg. He was working on his attitude, but still had trouble totally forgiving the mule for worsening his leg injury.

Teaching forgiveness came straight from God's Word. The owners of the boys' ranch preached on the topic often as they dealt with a group of rowdy kids who often lacked basic manners. He'd been one of the worst after living free in the rodeo world. For a while, he'd been angry at God for taking his mom. Eventually, he forgave the Lord, freeing him to remember the good times they'd shared as a family of two.

Anger reared its head again when he discovered he had an older sister that Mom had never mentioned. That situation left him with doubts about whether Mom failed to tell him about other relatives. Tamera had assured him she was the only sibling. Forgiving his mom made having a sister something he treasured from the time she started working at the ranch and through his recovery during the last year. Forgiving Sylvester and Leah would only bring blessings if he could get over the constant reminder from his weak leg. He had plenty of thinking to do as he traveled toward their destination.

When they neared the final turn, he reached out and laid a hand on Leah's shoulder. "It's time to wake up. We're almost there."

She stretched and peered out the window. "It looks like the place the farmer described to Shannon."

Carlton noted that one side of the road contained wide-open fields full of growing crops. Across the road, factories and warehouses stood in stark contrast. "I wonder if your mule was housed in one of those buildings. There's a few that resemble pole barns."

"That's a possibility. Slow down. I want to get the names of the businesses so I can research them." Leah pulled out her phone and started snapping pictures.

"We're nearing the farmer's house. Do you want me to pull in, or do you want to keep collecting business names?" Carlton slowed his SUV.

"Let's go on for a bit. Shannon mentioned the farmer initially spotted Sylvester on the north end of his property."

Carlton continued down the road until they came to another farmhouse. No other factories lined the road beyond that point. "It looks like this is the end of our farmer's property. Let's go talk to him."

"That sounds good. I'm going to make sure I got a clear photo of the business names." Leah hovered over her phone, flipping from one photo to the next.

As he drove back toward the farm, he noticed a man standing outside one of the barn-like buildings, watching as they came closer. The guy shielded his eyes and then ducked inside before Carlton could identify any features. The person's build was similar to the pharaoh at the comic convention, but he couldn't be sure without a closer look. This was one time he wished Kent had been in business long enough to have a few business vehicles. The crooks definitely knew his by now.

"Did you get a good photo of Remington Labs?" he asked.

"I did." She raised her eyebrows.

"That one might be the first one to research. There was a guy outside that was watching us." Seconds later, he steered his vehicle into a circular driveway leading them to a red barn behind a white Craftsman-style farmhouse. Three horses stood near a fence with leads tied to a top rail. They were equipped with full tack and ready to ride.

The farmer approached them with his hand held out. "You must be Leah and Carlton. My name's Bob Walton." He shook their hands. "If you want to see where I found that ornery mule, it is easiest to travel on horseback. I've got over two hundred acres and some places are back from the road. Are you both riders?"

"Yes," Carlton answered as Leah nodded.

The farmer looked at the cane Carlton leaned on and raised his eyebrows.

Carlton jutted out his chin. "If you have a mounting block, I'll be fine. I've ridden all my life."

"Not a problem, since I have to use one myself these days. This brown Morgan is Henry, and the small palomino is Chester. You two can ride them. Greta's my gal." Smashing a straw hat on his head, Bob led his dappled gray mare inside a corral where a two-step cement block stood. They followed, leading their mounts and took turns getting in the saddles.

Carlton noticed a rifle attached to Bob's saddle. "Nice weapon. I learned to use one like it when I was a teen. Do you expect trouble?"

"No. I always come prepared for snakes, reptiles or humans." Bob patted the weapon's holder.

Carlton nodded. "Good idea. Just remember snakes will bite if you aren't careful."

The farmer chuckled. "I mainly use my rifle to scare critters away from where they don't belong."

Leah spoke for the first time. "I hope you didn't use your gun on my mule."

"Nah. I didn't want him tearing up my field any more than he had. I herded his sorry carcass back toward the road. I didn't figure he'd go far based on how scrawny he was, but he took off before I could catch him. That's when I called the Humane Society about helping me round him up. When I heard they gave him to an auction house, I figured he was a goner. I'm glad you gave him a home."

"I am too. How far is it to where you first found him?" Leah straightened in her saddle.

"We'll be there in about fifteen minutes. You'll know you're there when you see where that mule destroyed part of my crop several months ago."

They rode on in silence through tall corn, until Carlton noticed an open area. The lack of growth made it clear that Sylvester had wreaked havoc on the first growth in the farmer's field.

Bob reined in closer. "There you go. I don't know what you'll spot that I didn't. Of course, I wasn't looking for anything other than the best way to get him away without doing more harm."

Carlton leaned low in the saddle and searched the ground. "When you found the mule, could you tell which direction he came from?" He noticed a slight divide in the crop, indicating a possible trail.

Bob rode closer and looked where Carlton stared. "What do you know? That sure looks like a trail back to the road. I think I herded the mule that way. Over yonder is where I got him moving." He pointed to another path-like gap. "Do you think someone dropped him off?"

"Either that or he came from one of the factories across the way. Have you ever seen any animals in those buildings?" Carlton's thoughts slipped back to Remington Labs.

"Not to my knowledge. I was disgusted when the neighbors sold their farmlands to the big corporations. Those buildings put out plenty of noise, and steam gushes out of their chimneys. I don't think critters would put up with being inside. My livestock aren't real happy as it is. I'm glad my barn is behind the home place."

As Carlton listened, a distant buzzing sound grew louder. The three riders twisted in their saddles, trying to locate the source. A shadow crossed the ground as a drone hovered overhead. It bobbed closer to each person and then backed away. Greta and Chester neighed as they danced across the open part of the field. Henry held steady and stood his ground, giving Carlton an idea.

Carlton nudged Henry closer to Bob. "Mind if I borrow your gun? I'd love to shoot him down, but legally I can't. Maybe I'll bluff him into thinking he's under threat."

Chapter Ten

Leah nudged her horse away from the other two. The drone made Chester skittish. Carlton adding the possibility of gunshot to the mix spelled trouble. "Shooting from the back of a horse isn't wise."

Bob laughed as he offered the gun to Carlton. "Henry is retired military. There ain't much that affects that horse."

Leah spoke calming words and rubbed a soothing circle on the side of Chester's neck while Carlton pointed the gun directly at the drone. Chester's head jerked upward when the drone dived away. Once the drone no longer hovered overhead, Carlton fired the gun toward the ground. The horse didn't run. The drone zoomed across the field and ran into an electric line before it tumbled from the sky.

"Good idea, man. He did his own damage. Shall we go retrieve that contraption?" Farmer Bob started guiding Greta down the left trail. Carlton followed.

Leah decided to join them when fear tightened her shoulders. She wasn't one to crave being with others, but this wasn't the time to be left alone. Carlton's threat had taken the drone down without violating the law. The rifle sitting across his lap demonstrated his talent for using the weapon. So far, the people threatening her hadn't resorted to weapons. She prayed the drone didn't prove otherwise when they found it.

"Where do you think it landed?"

"It has to be somewhere next to the electric wire it tangled with." Carlton's voice drifted back as they followed single file in the direction Bob led. About ten minutes later, they stopped near the edge of Walton property and circled their mounts. A few scrap pieces of metal and plastic lay beside several trampled plants.

"I guess whoever was at the controls got here before we did." Leah slid from her horse's back and stooped to look at the broken pieces. "Should we gather these scraps for evidence, or wait for the police?"

Carlton's gaze roamed over the area. "I don't like that we're out in the open. The people wanting to come after you could be in any of those buildings. We should probably get back to the farmhouse first."

Bob nodded. "Since it was on my property, I can talk to the police once we're safe inside."

Leah put her hands on her hips. "I don't like being stalked. Give me a couple of seconds to at least take some pictures with my phone."

"Make it quick." Carlton didn't sound happy.

Leah finished her task and mounted Chester. "Let's get back to safety." She followed Carlton between swishing rows of corn and couldn't help admiring his ability to ride Henry.

Once they reached the farmhouse, Bob led the procession to the block and dismounted.

Carlton waved her ahead. "You did pretty good getting on and off your horse back there in the field." His words bolstered Leah's confidence in her abilities to work with equines.

"Every day that I'm not on tour, I work with my mules. Mounts and dismounts are part of my normal routine. I'll be glad to get back home." She stepped down the stairs and led Chester out of the way.

Carlton edged Henry closer to the mounting block. "We'll get you home once we're sure it's safe. I was glad to be on a well-trained horse today."

"You ride well yourself, Cowboy." Heat warmed her neck. She prayed he couldn't see the pink that surely flooded her cheeks. For now, he had his back turned as he slid from Henry's saddle.

"Like I said, I grew up on a ranch and now my sister provides horse therapy at the place." He shook his head and turned her way with a wry smile on his face. "I see you haven't forgotten my nickname."

"Today you lived up to your alias. Your riding ability is cowboy worthy." So was his skill deceiving the drone operator by aiming and then shooting at the ground, from horseback, once they weren't being watched. She bit her tongue to keep from complimenting him more. Something about the man made her spew out more words than she normally spoke in public. She needed to change the subject before she totally embarrassed herself. "I remember Tamera's property shares a border with my ranch. I assume that's where you grew up."

"Yeah." A slight frown flickered across his face, before settling into a neutral expression. "Let's get these horses to the barn for a rubdown. They need to be taken care of, so they don't run away like a certain mule." The last part came out softer and gruffer than the rest of his comment.

"Okay..." Leah wondered what she'd done to upset the man again. Did he still resent Sylvester causing his injury? She swallowed. Having a limp for life would be an adjustment for anyone. Particularly for a man who had been an agent for federal law enforcement.

She could understand why Kent retired at an age-appropriate time in his life and started a new venture. Realizing her mule caused a major redirection in Carlton's life suddenly weighed heavy on her conscience. He'd mentioned the accident briefly, but hadn't spoken about the incident again. Having to protect her must be trying.

Bob directed them to adjoining stalls where they removed tack and groomed their rides. An occasional snort from the horses, and Bob's voice as he called 911, provided brief interruptions but didn't break the heavy silence hanging in the air.

Leah shook her head. The man was brooding. She didn't need that in her life. The one man she'd liked as a younger woman had betrayed her. Having someone who had doubts about working for her wasn't what she needed. She had to clear the air.

Securing Chester in his stall, she stepped over to the next stall and peered inside. She spoke as Carlton still worked with Henry.

"Look, I'm sorry that Sylvester had a part in your injuries. That doesn't mean you need to wallow in self-pity the rest of your life, or resent my mules. If you have a problem with that, then Kent needs to assign a different bodyguard. I'm not sure I can rely on my agent right now. I need to know if I can trust you to get over your resentment enough to respect me." Leah couldn't believe she'd spoken so many words, but saying them made her feel better. She rolled her shoulders and stood taller.

~~~~~

Carlton stared at the woman in disbelief. In the last few hours, he'd driven her where she wanted to go, faced down a drone that tormented them in the middle of a cornfield, and now he had to endure her sharp tongue. That didn't even include dealing with pharaohs, mummies, reckless drivers, and a sleep-deprived night. What a change from the woman who'd barely spoken during their first meeting.

He shook his head. She wasn't going to know the other half of what that wild mule had taken from him. Sharing the consequences with her or any woman was the last thing he wanted to do. When he presented the problem before, his former fiancée had dropped him like a burning coal and returned the ring. He turned to give Henry one more swipe with the brush, biding his time so he wouldn't say something he'd regret.

A sigh came from outside the stall. "Sorry. I'm so frustrated right now with this whole situation. I apologize again for any injuries Sylvester caused. Kent failed to let me know my mule did any harm to you. Sylvester wasn't sure what to do the first few weeks we had him. He ran away several times. We've been working on gaining his trust and even taught some basic commands before he developed the recent infection. That's when the doctor discovered Sylvester had something under his skin." She paused. "I'd like to go see Sylvester at the veterinarian and the rest of my mules at the farm as soon as we're finished reporting the drone incident."

"That's not a good idea. Taking Kent and Winnie's offer for staying
~~~~~

at their place would be the best thing for tonight. You'll be safe there. They have a great security system, and Kent was a top-notch agent when he worked for the feds." And Carlton needed a good night's sleep at his own place.

He took his cane from where he'd hooked it over the door and made his way out of Henry's stall. The crunch of gravel in Bob's drive indicated another vehicle had arrived. Stepping from the barn, he spotted a female deputy getting out of her car. Leah followed him to where they met Bob in his yard.

After reporting what happened and sharing Leah's photos, they left the farmer to show the deputy the drone's crash site. The officer pointed out one thing Carlton hadn't brought up. How did the people following Leah know where they were? He had no idea unless they'd randomly spotted their car going down the road where the culprits had once searched for Sylvester.

As they drove back to the Russell home, Carlton watched for both automobile and drone followers. He was relieved when no one appeared to be trailing them and that Leah napped, or at least appeared to do so. He still had a lot to think about. Maybe she wasn't directly at fault, but the mule had changed his life and ruined his relationship with one woman. He blew out a huff of air. She was right about one thing. His thoughts were dragging him into a pity party he needed to avoid. Winnie had already lectured him on that topic. *Help me, Lord. You spared my life when it could have been worse. Forgive me and help me forgive others.*

The setting sun colored the sky with a blaze of crimson. He was blessed to be alive. The accidents with the criminals and the mule could have done more than cripple his leg. Reaching out, he touched Leah's hand. Warmth he should not be feeling shot up his arm.

He cleared his throat as she awoke. "You're right. I accept your apology, and I need to get over myself. No more pity parties, but I am a work in progress. I have to move forward and be grateful for the abilities I have, as best as I can."

She gave his hand a squeeze, sending a message straight to his heart. "One of your abilities is riding, Cowboy. Are you sure we can't stop by the ranch? You could take a ride on one of my mules."

"The answer is no to going to the mule ranch. I'll stick to horses." He pulled his hand away and tried to concentrate on driving.

"Take it from one who has been on both types of equines, my babies provide a much smoother ride." Her musical laugh tickled his ears enough to make him grin.

"Babies? It sounds like you have adopted them as your children." He took his gaze from the road for a split second to look at her. The glow of the setting sun rested on her cheeks.

"I have. They're my family." Her fingers tapped on the console between them. "Most people don't know I was adopted. Taking in and rehabilitating mules is my way of giving back."

"You were blessed to have someone adopt you. Mr. and Mrs. Dudley, who ran the boys' ranch, were my family. They took in my sister when she offered to work as a cook so she could be near me. We kept in contact until they passed. Do you have a close relationship with your parents?"

"Mom and I were close until she passed away several years ago. Dad and I are not anymore. He isn't happy that I don't want people to know we are related. He's a horse man like you and thinks I'm wasting time and money on mules." She crossed her arms.

Carlton passed a slow-moving car as silent tension invaded the car. "Sorry."

"There's nothing you can do about it. He and I can be stubborn people."

Carlton signaled his turn into the Russells' drive. "Okay... I see Winnie at the door. I'm sure you'll get plenty of mothering tonight."

"Aren't you staying?" Leah's eyebrows rose.

"I need to go home tonight to get some sleep and fresh clothing for tomorrow." Was it his imagination, or did she look sad that he wouldn't be staying?

"I'll miss having you around." Her voice wavered.

He'd miss her too. "No worries. I'll be back early tomorrow morning. Let me get your door." Carlton pulled himself from the car, and using the vehicle for support went to open her door. When he offered his hand, she took it and smiled. They headed to the trunk where he pulled out her suitcase. "Do you need the author box for tonight?"

"No. Leave it in your trunk for now."

"Don't you two look cute." Winnie's voice made Carlton take a step back from Leah.

"I'll take your suitcase up to the house," Kent offered. He had followed his wife to the car.

"We'd be happy to invite both of you for dessert or snacking on the leftovers from lunch." Winnie's warm invitation was tempting, but Carlton headed back to the driver's side of his car.

"Thanks, but I need to get back to my place and catch some sleep. I'll be here first thing tomorrow morning to take over my duties." Carlton also needed time to sort out the feelings that were arcing between him and Leah. "See you then." He slid into his seat as the others headed toward the house. Leah looked over her shoulder and sent him a shy grin. He needed to get a grip if he was going to keep his head clear enough to provide protection for the beautiful woman.

He headed to the small cottage he rented on the outskirts of town. Tamera had offered him a place to stay on the ranch, but it was an hour drive from Forest Glen and Guardians Security. He also wanted to show the world he could make it on his own and not rely on his big sister's help. He parked in the drive and headed inside for a warm shower.

Afterward, he crashed onto his leather recliner with a bag of microwave popcorn and clicked on the evening news. A city reporter briefly mentioned the mishap at the convention the day before, where an unidentified attacker came after an author with a knife. He was thankful the reporter didn't mention Leah or him. Pulling a sports throw over his body, he decided to rest his eyes for a few moments.

Crash.

Carlton woke with a jerk, threw off the cover, and eased to the floor. His front windowpane was shattered. A huge rock sat on broken glass. Paper wrapped around the stone revealed words in bright red letters. He retrieved his cane and fished the message closer. Breaking the painter's tape revealed a message.

We know you're in there, Mara. Make it easy and tell us where to find the mule by calling the number below by tomorrow morning. Otherwise, we'll keep coming after you. We know how to track your every movement.

Carlton frowned at the printed phone number, probably a burner. The crooks must have managed to put another tracker on his SUV and figured Leah was with him. At least she was safe for the night. So much for a good night's sleep... He found a piece of cardboard in his recycler and taped his window closed. The landlord wasn't going to be happy. Neither would Leah and Kent.

Chapter Eleven

Leah took a deep breath as the scent of frying bacon pulled her from a sound sleep. She'd slept well in the Russells' guest room. Shelves of children's books and toys lined the walls, indicating their grandchildren used the room when visiting. She sat up and reached for the sketchpad lying on the nightstand. Winnie had joined her for an hour of random sketching the evening before after snacking on leftovers. It was fun to create in the company of another artist without a deadline or required characters.

She'd drawn a few mules at first, then flowers in shaded vases. Her last doodles of the night revealed a caricature of a cowboy on a galloping mule. Winnie had noticed the resemblance to Carlton, and they'd both had a good laugh. A rumble from Leah's tummy reminded her about the bacon. Would Carlton eat breakfast at the Russells' home? Pulling on a pair of jeans and a tee shirt, she decided to find out as she followed her nose to the kitchen.

"Morning, magpie. I hope you like bacon, scrambled eggs, and cinnamon toast." Winnie stood beside the stove minding the bacon as she cracked eggs into a bowl. A cookie sheet of buttered bread sprinkled with cinnamon and sugar sat on an opposite countertop, ready for toasting under the broiler.

"Perfect." Leah swiveled her head toward the dining room. Winnie had plates and silverware already in place. Though there were four place settings, there was no sign of the person she hoped to see.

Winnie chuckled. "If you're looking for Carlton, he's in the den with Kent. The last I checked, he was snoozing." She paused from breaking eggs and turned to face Leah. Her expression sobered. "There was an incident at Carlton's place last night."

"Oh, no. Was he hurt?" Her heart sank in her chest.

"He's fine other than not getting the good night's sleep he was hoping for." Winnie relayed the information about the message-wrapped rock breaking Carlton's window, while she lifted bacon onto a warming plate and poured most of the grease into a metal bowl. "He found another tracking device under the bumper of his SUV. Before he fell asleep, he and Kent were plotting strategies for keeping you safe."

"I hope they're including my mules in their plans, especially Sylvester." Leah sat on a nearby stool. Concerns about her herd tied her gut in a knot.

"I'm sure they'll keep your animals in mind." Winnie placed the prepared bread in the oven and dumped the bowl of eggs into the hot skillet. Within a couple of minutes, the eggs were scrambled, the bread toasted, and the warm bacon was ready for the table. "Would you call the guys to breakfast, please?"

By the time Leah took a step toward the doorway, both men arrived in the kitchen and offered to carry the warm food to the table. The smell of hand soap mingled in the air with the breakfast aroma, reminding Leah to wash her own hands. She took care of that necessity and then carried in cartons of milk and orange juice while Winnie lifted a carafe of coffee from its base and headed for the dining room. After a quick blessing, they all loaded their plates and began eating.

Leah paused between bites of soft scrambled eggs. "I heard about the message. Do you think destroying another tracking device will keep the bad guys off my trail?"

"There's no guarantee, but at least we've eliminated one source." Carlton lifted a napkin to his chin and wiped away a drip of cinnamon-laced butter. A hint of bags beneath his eyes didn't detract from his handsome appearance.

"We also have a phone number. I'll check if some of my federal connections can do us a favor. Maybe they can track the device." Kent held a piece of bacon between his thumb and forefinger as he nibbled bites.

"I'd like to check on the ranch and Sylvester." Leah's fork clattered as she laid it down on her plate. Why were the men not seeing the urgency to find out his status at the vet's?

"Going there might lead those threatening you straight to your mule. Since Kent knows where your ranch is located, we decided he could go check things out this afternoon. You can let your ranch supervisor know he's coming and ask her to call the veterinarian for a report. That's the best we can do for now." Carlton crossed his arms and leaned back in his chair.

"What should I do in the meantime?" Leah didn't like the idea of sitting and waiting. She was used to days crammed with chores in the barn and working in her home studio on her creations.

"You could always stay here and spend time on your drawings for your next book. I'm sure Winnie would be willing to share her computer setup with you." Kent looked at his wife. She nodded in agreement.

"Thank you, but I'd like to be with my mules. They're my inspiration for my syndicated comic strip and the next graphic novel." A wave of homesickness tightened Leah's throat. The breakfast that made her mouth water minutes ago now tasted like sawdust.

"You're safer here." Carlton's voice brooked no argument.

"What about my lunch meeting with Penny?" Leah knew she was reaching for straws. Meeting Penny wasn't on her list of favorite things to do. Shoveling mule manure had more appeal.

"Did she mention where you were going?" Winnie asked.

"She said it was a surprise, someplace special she was offering as an apology for her attitude the last couple of months. I assume she'll send the information sometime this morning." Leah closed her eyes and took a calming breath.

"Are you sure you can trust Penny?" Winnie's soothing voice pierced her thoughts, leaving her with more doubts than she already had.

"I don't know for sure, but other than intense pressure to increase our sales, she's done her job well. I'd like to hear her explanation for pushing so hard and go back to the relationship we had when she started as my agent." Leah reached for the phone she normally had in her pocket. It wasn't there. Kent and Carlton had suggested she leave the cell turned off. The device currently resided in her purse in the bedroom. "If you'll excuse me, I should probably send her a text and see where we're meeting."

"No." Both men spoke at the same time.

"Send her an email using Winnie's computer. Tell her we're going to church this morning, and you'll meet her after noon." Kent finished off his last bit of toast and stood. "While you're sending the message, we all need to get dressed and head out."

"I'm not sure about going to church today." Carlton frowned as he laid his napkin across an empty plate.

Leah shuddered. "I could stay here and work on my art. I didn't bring any dresses." She'd not been in a public worship service in years. The crowd at the comic convention had worn her nerves thin. Sunday morning devotions hosted by one of her ranch hands had sufficed since she had started the rescue facility. She worshiped God on her own and in familiar small groups.

Winnie sat her coffee cup down and glanced at Leah and Carlton. "We're not accepting excuses. We need God's help for this situation. Worshiping is one way to show our gratitude." The determined look on her face said there wasn't a choice.

"But the clothing..." Leah swallowed and looked down at her jeans and tee shirt.

"Our church dresses casually. That won't be an issue. Besides, I know everyone will be glad to see Carlton back where he belongs."

Winnie gathered empty dishes and headed into the kitchen before Leah could come up with another excuse.

Carlton looked like he'd been hog-tied and dragged across rough terrain. Leah wanted to run and hide.

~~~~~

Discomfort crawled over Carlton like a wandering tick as he entered the sanctuary of Forest Glen's Church of the Rock. He and God had a lukewarm relationship right now. He prayed when he needed something, but more often than not, he couldn't help wondering why God had taken away so much. Besides having a lame leg, the woman he thought he loved ended their relationship over other changes. It didn't help that he'd probably see his former fiancée when the song service ended.

In the past his ex had always herded the kids out for children's church. She loved the little ones and wanted several of her own. When Carlton suggested adoption, she'd said it wouldn't be the same. Her love for him wasn't enough if he couldn't give her the descendants she wanted to carry on her family's bloodlines. Not many people knew of that complication from his wounds.

Winnie had mentioned the woman was now dating a man who started attending in the last few months. His ex had moved on. Why couldn't he? He knew the answer but had mixed feelings about forgiveness. Maybe he was wallowing in a pity party. A clap on his back tossed his wandering thoughts to the nearest pew.

"Hey, stranger. It's good to see you back in the Lord's house. We've missed having you around."

He automatically offered his right hand to one of the deacons standing just inside the doors.

Clasping the man's hand warmed Carlton's heart and soul. "Thanks, Ben. It's good to see you too." The man's greeting reminded him that fellowship with people at the church was something he'd really missed.

"There's a men's fellowship next weekend. We'd be glad to have you." Ben handed him a bulletin and pointed to the information about the outing.

"I'm on a case right now for Guardians Security Group." He waved toward the Russells and Leah. His beautiful client was staring at the stained-glass windows and practically leaning on Winnie. "I'll keep the event in mind if things wrap up soon."

Stepping away from his friend, he slipped his hand through Leah's elbow as they followed Winnie and Kent down the main aisle. He pulled her closer when his ex-fiancée nodded in his direction. The woman's
~~~~~

mouth gaped. Let her think what she wanted. He looked away and wrapped an arm across Leah's shoulders as they slid into a pew. Maybe his ex would get the wrong idea. He hoped Leah didn't, as her eyes opened wide.

"Are you all right? I was only trying to show you where to sit." He might have imagined it, but he thought she shivered.

"I'm not used to large crowds. That's one of the reasons the comic convention made me nervous. Worshiping God on the ranch is small and simple with only a few people attending."

Leah's response was quiet enough that he leaned closer to hear. Leaving his arm across the back of the seat seemed the natural thing to do. Winnie's lavender-scented soap smelled better on Leah than it did on her hostess.

"I haven't attended here much since my injury, but I think you'll like our song leaders. They aren't too loud, and the songs are easy to sing. Concentrate on them and not the full room of people. Everyone is here to worship God." He squirmed at his hypocrisy. Sounding like a preacher wasn't the message he should convey with anger still stirring up his soul.

After a call to worship, everyone stood and sang with the praise band. Carlton's tongue loosened. He started singing along and relaxed as his voice rose in songs of praise.

Leah leaned next to him after they sat. She picked up a pew pencil and wrote on the edge of her bulletin.

Nice voice. You're full of hidden talents.

He shook his head and relaxed until the preacher started talking about forgiveness. Pastor Kaleb had been the assistant last time Carlton had been in church. Now he was leading the congregation and his direct look made Carlton squirm. Pulling his arm from the back of the pew, he hunched over his knees and half-way listened to the sermon as he prayed for the peace that eluded him. Leah's hand on his elbow brought some comfort, even though it reminded him of the mule that dealt the last blow to his wounded body.

When they stood for the final hymn, leaving was all he wanted, which would have happened if Winnie and Kent hadn't stood in the way. As soon as a path cleared, he led Leah toward his SUV. He blew out a heavy breath as they approached the passenger door.

"Is there something you'd like to talk about?" She looked as relieved as he did about getting to their vehicle.

"Not really. I need to deal with things from my past on my own. Are you ready to head back to Kent's to figure out your lunch plans?"

"Sure." She climbed into the passenger's side while he waited to close the door.

Leah settled in her seat and then pointed. "Is there something under your wiper?"

Carlton closed her door and limped to the other side of his vehicle. He lifted the wiper holding down a paper fluttering in the breeze. He picked it up between two fingers and glared at the message.

We told you we'd be watching. Time is running out.

Chapter Twelve

Leah watched as a frown wrinkled Carlton's brow. Had they received another threat? "What is it?"

He leaned into the front seat and held the threatening note just out of her reach, but close enough to read. "Somehow, they are still keeping up with us. Whether it was knowledge of Kent going to church here or another tracker, I have no idea. We should cancel with Penny."

"Since they know our location, I'm going to turn on my phone to contact her." She pulled her phone out and revived it. Various notifications pinged. Instead of checking them, she went straight to the calling function.

"Fine. I'm going to look for another tracker." He placed the note on the dashboard and worked his way around the SUV.

Leah dialed Penny's number. The agent answered on the third ring.

"Hey, Leah. Are you ready to go to the best restaurant I could find in this small burg?" Excitement resonated in Penny's voice as she named off one of Leah's favorites. Leah's mouth watered. Though she'd never been inside the popular restaurant because of her reclusive habits, she often asked Shannon to bring carry-out to warm up at the ranch. Penny would be surprised if she knew they were within an hour of the mule rescue ranch and that Leah considered Forest Glen more than a burg.

"Shirley's Sirloin Bistro sounds delicious. I saw their sign earlier today." She didn't need to admit about wondering if they could grab something there while they were in town. "Let me check with my bodyguard. Someone is still threatening me." She muted her phone and climbed out of the SUV. "Penny has offered to take us out to Shirley's. It's just around the corner from here. We could leave your vehicle and walk so no one could track us."

"I could use a meal at Shirley's. Let's leave this tracker in place until we're done." He leaned over and pointed to a small device under the side of the car.

"Great." She turned her mute off and let Penny know they could be there in fifteen minutes. As she hung up, Winnie and Kent approached. "Hey, it looks like we're eating at Shirley's. Do you want to join us?"

"Actually, we were thinking about making a run out to your ranch to find out if everything is fine there," Kent said. "There's a fast-food restaurant on the way that we both love. After eating at Charley Burgers and going to the ranch, we might stop by Carlton's sister's ranch to ride horses for a bit."

"Could you take my author's box and suitcase to the ranch? Please ask Shannon if she can pack some clean clothes for me. I need more casual clothing." Leah looked forward to having more outfit choices if this went on for more than a day. Either that or she'd need to do laundry.

"We'd be glad to help you." He opened their trunk and helped transfer the box of author paraphernalia and suitcase. Leah waved to Winnie as they drove away.

"Let's go eat. I'm ready for a sirloin steak at your agent's expense." Carlton rubbed his flat stomach and offered her an elbow.

She placed her arm through his and they made their way down the sidewalk. Touching the handsome man was becoming easier. She enjoyed being close to Carlton. As they walked together, it crossed her mind that the stroll might bother his leg.

"Are you okay walking?"

"I'm fine." His voice came across as grumpy. "I'm getting used to my condition. I've been told that walking helps loosen things up."

"Then think on the positive for now and the steak we're about to eat." Leah leaned closer as they turned a corner. *Mmmm,* he wore nice-smelling aftershave. It reminded her of saddle leather.

"I hope the company we will be keeping won't sour the taste of the food." He looked down at her and smiled. They both stumbled but recovered without a mishap thanks to Carlton planting his cane to hold them both steady.

"It shouldn't be too bad. Penny was a great person to work with earlier in our relationship. I'm praying she wants to heal that divide with more encouraging words and less pressure." She released his elbow and took his hand when he offered it. His cheeks took on a ruddy hue. She could only imagine the pink covering her own as they rounded the corner leading to the restaurant's front door. Penny stood waiting with her eyebrows raised.

"I see you two are getting cozy." Penny's voice interrupted Leah's muddied thoughts. Her agent's bright yellow pantsuit gleamed in the sunlight. Stilettos clicked on the cement as she walked toward them. Leah stepped away from Carlton and headed for the door of the restaurant. She had no idea how to respond, so she didn't.

"After you." Carlton held the restaurant door open for the women. His voice sounded far from welcoming, and a scowl crossed his face as he stared at Penny.

It seemed he wasn't thrilled by the woman's comment either, though his hand did rest on the middle of Leah's back as they made their way to a table. Penny had called ahead and made a reservation, so they went right in without waiting in line. A waitress bustled over to hand them menus, then left after taking their drink orders.

Penny smiled, but it didn't quite reach her eyes. "I wanted to apologize for the way I've been pushing you. There have been some issues that have affected my attitude. My parents haven't been well and helping with their care and bills at the nursing home has been difficult. I've had a couple of writers drop me as their agent lately. Those things put me in financial straits, which should be resolved thanks to your graphic novel's success and the tour you finished. I want this meal to be a celebration for both of us."

"I'll keep your apology in mind. Next time something happens, please keep me informed about what is going on." Leah searched her agent's face until the woman nodded.

"I promise to keep you updated." Penny's shoulders lowered.

"Good. I need an agent who has my best interests in mind." Leah lifted her glass and took a sip as Penny started chatting about deadlines for the next graphic novel.

Leah noticed that Carlton appeared to be studying her and Penny. At one point a platinum blonde woman wearing heavy makeup walked past their table and leaned down to whisper in Penny's ear. They nodded in agreement with whatever the woman had shared and then Penny turned back to her meal. A brief frown had crossed her face before her forced smile returned.

"Who was that?" Carlton asked. He turned to watch the blonde as she walked away.

Penny waved a dismissive hand. "Regina." Her mouth clamped closed. Had her face paled? "Just an acquaintance letting me know there was an event I might be interested in. Now tell me about the latest chapter in the graphic novel you're working on."

An hour into the meal, Penny's phone pinged from where it sat on the table. Leah couldn't help noticing the start of the message marked as being from Regina. *They found it...*

Penny picked up the phone and checked the message. Leah watched as the woman's shoulders relaxed and a grin crossed her face.

"Good news?" Leah asked.

"The best." Penny lifted her glass in a mock toast and then looked away.

~~~~~

Carlton wondered what the agent meant by her exclamation about something being the best. "Did you sell another book for an author?"

"No. I received some good news concerning a matter that I'd rather
~~~~~

not discuss right now." Penny laid a hand on her stomach as she chewed a bite of steak and swallowed. "This is delicious. Not bad for a small-town dive."

Leah stiffened. Carlton gave her hand a squeeze under the table, figuring she was ready to defend the restaurant and reveal her ranch's proximity to it.

He took his own bite and hummed his satisfaction. "This place is one of my favorites. Their steaks are better than any I've had in the city, or the whole country, for that matter."

Leah's hand relaxed under his. "I agree. This steak is one of the tastiest I've ever had."

Penny shrugged. "If you say so..." She took several more bites, demonstrating her approval of the steak in front of her, despite her nonchalance. They ate in silence for several minutes, finishing off their meals by cleaning their plates. When they waved off desserts, the waitress provided Penny with the bill.

"Thank you for buying our steaks. You seem happier in the last few minutes." Leah looked at the agent.

"It was the least I could do. Thanks to your new book and mule, my financial situation is much improved. Make that, mule comic strip." Penny looked down at the bill and placed her credit card on top.

Carlton wondered why Penny followed the comic strip omission with a correction. Did she know more about Sylvester's situation than she was admitting? Something wasn't adding up. He was having doubts about the agent's loyalty to Leah.

Penny tapped her fingers on the table and looked around the room. "I like their decor. It's kind of like a ranch."

Carlton waited to see if the woman would mention the mule rescue ranch. When she didn't, he added, "This place reminds me of my home. I grew up around horses. Are you a rider?"

Penny shook her head. "I was never interested in putting my life at risk on the back of an animal." A shudder confirmed her dislike.

Then why had she been so interested in Leah's mules? After the waitress returned with her receipt and credit card, they stood and walked to the front door of the restaurant.

"Do you have any plans for this afternoon?" Penny asked.

"Not yet." Leah walked out ahead of the others and waited on the sidewalk.

"Would you like to visit the cabin I rented for the rest of my stay here in small-town America? There's a lake surrounded by a forest. It's very peaceful. There's even a place you can rent a horse to ride on trails." Penny seemed sincere, but Carlton didn't picture her as the type to rent a cabin in the woods.

"Thank you, but we need to take care of some issues with my SUV." Carlton started down the sidewalk toward the church. The woman didn't need to know he'd be searching for additional tracking devices.

"Where is your vehicle?" Penny followed them for several steps.

"We left it at the church located around the block." Leah pointed toward their destination.

"At least let me take you there so you don't have to walk so far." Penny's gaze turned to Carlton's leg and cane.

Discomfort and irritation boiled beneath the facade he displayed to the women.

"We'll be fine." He didn't need the agent's pity.

"I don't mind taking you there." Penny waved them toward her car. Leah grabbed his hand and followed her agent, leaving Carlton without a choice. He needed to stay with his client and there was no way he would trust Penny to keep her safe.

Leah climbed into the back. Carlton maneuvered into the passenger seat. After fastening his belt, he crossed his arms. Something didn't feel right. Then again, what could go wrong while going one block back to the church?

Plenty.

"Where is my car?" He gaped as Penny pulled into the church parking lot. No one else was there, not even his vehicle. He pulled out his phone and dialed 911.

City police arrived within a few minutes, took a description of the missing SUV, and left when a call about a wreck came over the radio. Carlton dialed Kent to update their situation. No one answered. Odd. Had his boss turned off his phone when they reached Leah's ranch? Carlton gripped the cell in his hand and stuffed it in his pocket.

"Would you like me to take you somewhere?" Penny's expression appeared open, but she was the one who'd been pleased about a development during their meal. Could the missing vehicle be a coincidence?

He studied the woman's face, looking to see any hint of deception.

"If you don't want my help, I understand, but I'd be glad to take you to my cabin where you can rest until you hear news from the police about your car. At least think of my client. She's had a rough week."

"Would it hurt to get away for a while?" A tired smile crossed Leah's face.

He frowned, still uncertain whether to trust Penny. "Where is this cabin located?"

"There's a campground about forty-five minutes west of here, called

Green Willow Lake. My cabin is there." The agent made direct eye-contact and didn't look away. At least that information was correct.

"I know the place. It's about fifteen minutes from my sister's horse therapy ranch. I'll let her know so she can pick us up." The location was also suspiciously close to Leah's mule ranch. Not trusting the woman was a good thing, but could he also use her ploy to create a double cross if the men who'd been harassing Leah were somehow in league with Penny?

He sent a text to his sister, who confirmed she could be at the campground in an hour.

When Penny didn't react to him sending his sister a text, he decided to take a chance on her offer. At least Tamera would know where to locate them.

"Let's go. My sister will meet us at the campground around the time we arrive."

As they climbed back into Penny's car, he sent a prayer heavenward. *Lord, protect us. I hope I've made the right decision. Keep Leah and my sister safe from harm.*

Chapter Thirteen

Leah watched the flat northern Ohio landscape blur outside the car window as they headed west toward Penny's rented cabin. No one followed. That was a relief. Even Carlton seemed to relax into his seat with his eyes closed as the miles passed. Penny's chatter about trying to find the best book deals for her clients during a recent trip to Chicago kept Leah awake.

"I thought the best publishing deals might be in New York." Leah broke into the one-sided conversation.

"Traditionally speaking, many are in New York, but there are also possibilities in Chicago and several places out west. I like going to the Big Apple or the Windy City. When I have the money, I can always catch a great musical or museum when I visit those cities." Penny's GPS indicated a turn, so she flipped on her blinker and exited the highway. "We're getting close to the cabin according to my device."

A wave of concern infiltrated Leah's thoughts. "Haven't you been to the Green Willow Camp before?"

"Good question, Leah." Carlton had apparently awakened when the car slowed.

Penny tapped a bright red fingernail on the steering wheel. "I rented the cabin for tonight without seeing the place, but I have it on good authority about the beautiful lake and horseback riding activities. A contact of mine assured me the cabin is perfect for a quiet getaway. Are you sure you don't want to check the place out while we wait on Carlton's sister?"

He leaned sideways in the front seat. "My sister, Tamera, should be there close to the time we arrive. We'll be on our way once she gets there. I'd like to do any horse riding at her place." His gaze met Leah's as he lifted his chin and gave a small shake of his head.

She guessed he wasn't comfortable being under Penny's control any more than she. "Yes. I can hardly wait to see Tamera's horse therapy ranch. Maybe I'll get some new inspiration for my writing and illustrations."

Penny turned onto a smaller road with a sign indicating the camp was another mile away. "My invitation is open if you change your mind."

Carlton's phone pinged with a text message. A frown marred his face as he typed a response.

"Is something wrong?" Leah leaned forward from the backseat.

"Tamera's horses are loose. She'll be here as soon as she rounds them up. It looks like someone opened the corral gate, which doesn't make any sense. She's usually the only one around on Sundays, and she wouldn't be that careless with her animals." Carlton tapped on his phone. Leah couldn't help but wonder what he was telling his sister.

"Then you'll be able to stay and enjoy the cabin for a while." Exuberance poured from Penny's voice.

Leah was tired of Penny's pushing and needed to know if there was an ulterior motive. "Why do you want us to go to the cabin with you?"

"Is offering you something nice a crime? I just wanted you to have some time to relax after enduring the tour. I know it wasn't something you enjoyed. I'm sorry the event was so stressful for you. Coming here is one way I can apologize for all you went through. We can celebrate our success." The literary agent drove through the arched entrance to the camping area without adding to her declaration.

Penny parked next to the last cabin at the end of a road. "At least come in and visit until Tamera rounds up her horses. The key is supposed to be in the door."

Leah stretched as she climbed from the cramped backseat and walked toward the building. Carlton walked to one side of the chalet-style log structure. He appeared to be inspecting the exterior, before turning to observe the promised lake spreading out beyond the forested backyard. A trail twisted through the trees toward a short dock jutting into the water. She edged near him, feeling unsure about going inside the cabin.

He leaned his head to one side and took Leah's hand. "A walk down to the lake might be relaxing. Do you want to join us, Penny?"

"Thank you, but I have a call to make. You two enjoy some well-deserved downtime." The Cheshire cat grin spreading across her agent's face didn't encourage any trust on Leah's part.

"We won't be gone long." They watched Penny sit in one of the Adirondack chairs on the cabin's front porch before heading toward the lake.

"Should we make a run for it?" Leah fought the panic rising in her chest.

"Let's circle around the edge of the building and see if we can catch any of her conversation before we make a move. I've already texted Tamera not to come until I tell her otherwise." He laid a finger across his lips as they made their way to the far side of the chalet.

Penny's angry voice quieted any natural sounds from the park environment. "I did what you said. What do you mean the mule wasn't at her ranch? The problems you ran into at that location are yours, not mine. Just pay me what you owe for my part in this. I want out. Yeah, they're here, but I'm not sure how long I can keep them, unless you do something else to delay the sister."

Leah clamped a hand over her mouth. Something was definitely wrong. It sounded like they'd gone to her ranch to find Sylvester.

Carlton waved her toward a different trail than the one leading to the lake. His commanding voice whispered close to her ear. "Come on. When I was one of the ranch kids, we cleared trails for this place for a summer project. We're going to borrow some horses and get out of here while we can. If I remember correctly, there's a power line path that runs along the back of this property. It connects to the edge of the state park. I'll have Tamera meet us with a horse trailer in the park."

As they hurried down the trail, Carlton called his sister and let her know to meet them at a different place. "Can you give Jim a call? We're going to borrow some horses and get there as soon as we can."

"Won't the owner of the stable think we've stolen his horses?" Leah followed Carlton through the opening in the woods. Her breath came fast. He made good time, despite using a cane.

"I used to know Jim. He runs the stables here. If he's around and Tamara catches him on the phone, taking the horses won't be a problem." Carlton waved Leah to a stop when a red barn came into view.

"Do you see your friend?" Leah peered around him and spotted a huge guy arguing with a man in western gear. "That doesn't look good."

~~~~~

"Let's see what happens." Carlton stepped back into the trees, drawing Leah with him. Sinking to the ground was awkward, but he did it for the sake of hiding. He could make out angry voices, but not their exact words. He closed his eyes to concentrate and catch his breath from their rush through the forest.

When the shouting ended, Leah started to rise. He reached out and pulled her down as he mouthed "wait." A minute later, an engine roared to life. Carlton rolled to one side and peered through the brush. The lone figure of a wrangler stood next to a pair of horses tied to a hitching post. When the cowboy made no move to take the horses into their barn, Carlton watched the fellow wave his hat in the air and give a loud whistle. The horses shook their heads but didn't react otherwise. Carlton recognized the familiar signal. He twisted up to his knees and then pushed into a standing position.

"It appears that Tamera let our mutual friend know we need rides. Sorry, no mule, but Jim always has a good string of horses." Carlton worked his way closer to the saddled mounts, keeping alert for any
~~~~~

trouble. Leah followed close enough behind him to have a hand on the back of his shirt. They approached the horses and adjusted the stirrups. Leah scrambled into her saddle, while Jim stepped from the shadows at the last minute to boost Carlton into place.

"Thanks, Jim. I'm glad you were on duty today."

"No problem. It's good to see you back in the saddle again. Tamera said she'd be at the Roger's Inlet parking lot in an hour. You sure you don't want me to just run you over in the truck?" the wrangler said.

"We're avoiding the road for now. Thanks for the offer."

"I can't blame you. That excuse for a man that just left was meaner than a rattlesnake. He wanted to know why I had two horses ready. I told him I always have a couple of rides saddled for tourists, which is the truth on a busy day. He started arguing with me when I said I hadn't seen you two. I told that guy to hit the trail, which didn't go over well."

"That's what I figured. We better get moving in case he decides to come back. Tamera will take care of these two horses until we connect again." Carlton nodded his thanks to Jim and guided the mare toward a path leading away from the lake. He looked back at Leah. "This passage bisects with the power line corridor I talked about. We should have an easy ride once we get there. The electric company tries to keep the brush cleared under the lines."

"Do you think we can make the rendezvous in an hour?" Her voice wavered.

"Tamera will wait for us if we run late." He had confidence his sister had already rounded up her missing horses and was hitching up a trailer to her farm truck.

"Won't that put her in danger?"

"I hope she has thought of contacting Kent. If so, they will be there too. He and Winnie planned to stop by Tamera's place after dropping off your things at the mule ranch." He frowned. He wondered why Kent hadn't been bombarding him with texts or calls. Sharing that lack of communication with Leah might upset her even more, but he was beginning to wonder if his boss was okay.

"What if Kent and Winnie didn't make it to Tamera's place? Penny referenced some kind of trouble. Could they have run into the bad guys at my ranch when they went to check on things there?" Panic quaked in Leah's voice as she pulled her mount abreast with his.

He had to wonder if she could read his mind.

"Let's ride faster while we're on a clean trail."

Carlton pressed his horse to keep pace with her mount until they reached the power line. A smaller trail, the width of a four-wheeler, ran along the edge of the passage, slowing their movement to a walk.

Urgency emanated from Leah's body language as she took the lead toward the park.

He needed to think of something to distract her. The horses were starting to act skittish. "What was your favorite part of the book tour?"

"When it ended." Her abrupt answer clued him into his lack of a successful distraction.

"Okay. Tell me about the mule you named your comic strip after. Was his name Marty?"

"I see what you're up to. I'll try to settle down."

He heard her inhale deeply and then release a puff of air.

Her action didn't convince him that she'd relaxed.

"Humor me and tell me more about that mule. I'd like to know."

"Fine. He was my first mule. He's pretty ancient now, but he lived up to his original name of Smarty Pants by playing tricks and being contrary. Marty became an important part of my life. He had a much smoother gait than any horse I ever rode. That mule surprised me when he allowed me to teach him all kinds of equestrian moves. Marty gave me affection I never received from my father.

"Mom was the one who pushed for my adoption. Dad just wanted someone to carry on the family name and had hoped for a boy when the adoption agency said they only had girls. When he discovered I had artistic talent and a sense of humor, we connected for a while. When I decided to use a pen name and make it on my own, his limited affection for me flew out the window."

Carlton shook his head. She'd gone down another tension-filled rabbit hole full of sad memories. "Have you been to the state park before? We used to come here and swim in the summer."

"No. My life was secluded as a child. Public parks are not a good idea for the family of a famous person. We lived in a different part of the country back then."

"Using a pen name should help with hiding your identity now. Maybe you can get out and explore things." Thoughts of taking her places around the country sounded appealing.

"That worked when I only had the comic strip. The graphic novel has my photo on the back cover. That means real fans have no trouble identifying me, like our crooks have done the last few days."

Carlton gave up trying to change the subject. They rode without talking while the power line hummed above their heads. When they arrived at the trail that led into the state park, he took the lead. Ten minutes later, he spotted Tamera sitting in her truck with an attached horse trailer. No one was with her.

He guided his horse near her open window. "Hey, sis. Have you

heard from Kent and Winnie?"
"No. I haven't been able to contact them either."

Chapter Fourteen

"We need to go to my ranch now." Leah slid off her horse and led it to the open ramp of the trailer. Her heart pounded as she led her mount inside and tied it in place, leaving it saddled. Striding out of the trailer, she reached for her phone and tried calling her forewoman Shannon and then Kent. A call to the ranch's landline went unanswered. She ran a hand across her forehead as her worry increased.

Tamera rounded the corner, leading the mare Carlton had ridden. "He's already in the driver's seat, ready to move out. Let's get this gal loaded, and we'll head for your place."

The knot in Leah's throat kept her from replying out loud. She nodded and helped Tamera lift the gate, locking the horses inside.

The next few moments crawled by at a snail's pace as she watched the speedometer stay near the posted limit. "Can't we go faster?"

"I'd love to, but we have to think about the horses' safety." Carlton slowed for a sharp turn in the road.

He was right, but her people and animals were not safe at the moment. Leah's fingers tensed and released multiple times as prayers flew up to God. *Guide us, Lord. Protect my friends and ranch hands. What is going on with these people making them want Sylvester?* She blew out a huff of air.

Tamera laid a hand on Leah's wrist. "Would you like me to pray with you?"

She shrugged, not sure how to respond to someone else praying with her. Since she didn't attend church, her worship was solitary for the most part. "I've been praying, but haven't gotten an immediate answer."

"God likes hearing from us when two or more offer the same requests." Tamera's voice was soothing. Leah nodded as the woman sandwiched her fidgeting fingers between her warm palms and bowed her head.

"Pray so I can hear, sis. Even though God and I haven't spoken on a regular basis lately, we can use some help right now." Carlton's eyes focused forward as he continued driving.

Tamera led them in prayer, asking for courage, calmness, and clear minds as they faced an unknown situation. Peace and strength enveloped Leah's thoughts.

As she opened her eyes, Carlton's voice interrupted the prayer.

"We're getting close to Tamera's place. I need you to direct me to the mule ranch entrance."

An idea crossed her mind. Was it an answer to prayer? She hoped so. "Go past the main entrance coming up. Turn at the next lane after that. It's the one running between Tamera's property and mine. I had the fence repaired between the two ranches with a gate after Sylvester's two escapes. We can access my property from there. If trouble is going on at the ranch, they won't expect us to arrive from the forested area behind my barn."

Carlton slowed but didn't look happy about the prospect of going down the once-abandoned road. "I'm aware of the connection. I was the one who cleared the road out enough to put the lane back into service. It's probably overgrown again."

Tamera laughed. "You'll be happy to know I've kept it mowed since then. I now offer an overnight tent camping experience for my riders and drive a supply truck on the road every few weeks. Thanks to the stake-out when Winnie had her troubles, there's a great place to turn around. Unfortunately, there's still a problem with cell phone connections."

Leah's mind began churning with ideas as Carlton made the turn and slowed for dips in the gravel road. "We could ride Jim's horses to the mule ranch while Tamera heads to her place. We'll call her once we assess what's going on with my ranch hands and the Russells to let her know if we need police backup."

"I can handle that." Tamera gave Leah a high five.

"Ladies, this isn't a fun outing for you two to play at rescuing the world. Even though your plan sounds feasible, we are dealing with real criminals." He pulled to a stop and frowned at the women.

"That's why we're at your command, little brother." A serious look crossed Tamera's face as she lifted a mock salute and exited the truck.

"I understand your concerns. I'm worried about this whole situation and feel guilty that I may have caused everything to happen. We're just reacting to the stress by attempting to gain some control with our ideas." Leah leaned into his side as sorrow washed over her.

His Adam's apple bobbed. She swallowed back an emotional tangle twisting in her chest. They were too close for comfort. She'd never been that forward with a man before, not even with the boyfriend who'd ended up kidnapping her. Embarrassment made her chest and face burn. A hasty exit was called for. Pushing her way across the seat, she climbed from the truck and hustled to help Tamera with the horses.

Tamera wore a grin as she handed a lead to Leah. "Here you go. Your ride was ready a few seconds ago, but I didn't want to interrupt anything with my brother. By the way, he's not dating anyone."

Leah ignored that. "How are we going to get Carlton back in the saddle?" Heat filled her face when Tamera laughed. "I meant is there a mounting block here that he can use?"

"I have a couple of tree stumps set up for my campers that will work for getting back on the horse." She leaned closer and lowered her voice as Carlton stepped from the truck. "You'll have to figure out on your own how to date my mulish brother."

~~~~~

Carlton was thankful for the stumps that provided crude mounting blocks for getting on the horse. He wasn't appreciative of the knowing looks his sister was throwing his and Leah's direction. Tamera definitely had other things on her mind than catching criminals and protecting the innocent. He needed to escape her matchmaking designs and get back to his bodyguard duties. Who was she, anyway, to consider promoting romance? Her last attempt at dating ended up in the kidnapping of a young girl in his protective care.

He focused his attention on following Leah through the gate to her property. She sat her horse well as they wove down a meandering trail. He admired her skill. When she slowed, he could see the ranch through the trees. A few mules wandered aimlessly in a corral near the barn. No people were visible. An abandoned straw hat sat in the grass outside the barn. Everything was quiet. Too quiet.

He watched Leah dismount and secure her gelding to a tree. He did the same after landing hard on his injured leg. He bit back a groan when he took his first step away from the horse. Grabbing his cane from where it dangled off the saddle, he followed her as they approached the barn, going from tree to bush. One of the mules in the corral lifted its nose in the air and bellowed out a whistling *hee-haw*. The other two joined with their brays. Leah held up a hand toward him. They both paused to see if anyone would come outside.

When the mules calmed down, he heard a faint cry for help. Leah started to rush ahead.

"Wait. Let me go first." He hobbled forward, searching from side to side as he entered the shadowed interior of the barn. Thumping sounds came from a stall to his left as he heard another call for help in a familiar voice.

"Is that you, boss?" Carlton stepped inside the barn.

"Yeah." Kent's voice sounded muffled. "Winnie and I are tied up next to an unconscious woman. I think all the crooks are gone."

Carlton entered the stall and released the couple while Leah bent over the injured woman.

"Wake up, Shannon. Are you all right? What happened?"
~~~~~

The woman moaned and muttered a single word as her brow creased. "Mules?"

Other than the three in the paddock, Carlton hadn't seen any mules. He watched as the realization flooded Leah's understanding.

"My mules. They've taken my mules." Her voice squeaked.

"Ran them off. Wanted Sylvester. Warn Doc." Shannon's eyes closed. Her chest continued to rise and fall, but she visibly needed help.

Carlton dialed 911 and reported the need for an ambulance as Leah knelt by her forewoman. Tears rolled down her face. He laid a hand on her shoulder. "If the mules just ran off, they'll come back, or we'll find them."

Winnie stepped between them and laid a saddle blanket over Shannon, who had started shivering. "Stay still. Help will be here soon." Her calming voice seemed to soothe the woman on the ground and the one kneeling nearby. "Is there anyone else we need to check on?"

Leah stood. "There's an older couple who stay at the house when I'm away. We need to find them. Paul's straw hat is out in the yard."

"Why don't you let Carlton and Kent make sure they are safe? Shannon needs you right now." Winnie held her hand out toward Leah, who looked conflicted.

Carlton stepped between Leah and the exit from the barn. "I'll go to the house. I think the worst is over, but I'd feel better if Kent stayed here until more help arrives."

He headed to the one-story ranch house. On the way there he stopped to pick up the fallen hat. When he arrived, he found the older couple tied to kitchen chairs. They were visibly upset but were not injured. He introduced himself as Leah's bodyguard as he placed the hat on the table and started untying their ropes.

"Why does she need a bodyguard?" the older man asked, after introducing himself as Paul.

"We've had some bad guys harassing Leah over the last few days. How many did you see when they tied you up? Do you have a description?"

"There were two inside with us, but we could hear someone else outside." The woman, who identified herself as Josephine, rubbed her released wrists together.

"The two in here wore ski masks. One of them smelled like a smoker." Paul stretched his legs and reached for the dusty hat.

Carlton clenched his fists. This was bigger than he'd thought. "There were only two men following us the other day."

"Is Miss Leah safe?" Josephine wrung her hands.

Carlton nodded. "She's fine. Shannon is injured. They're both in the barn. An ambulance should be here soon."

"I'll get your first-aid kit, honey." Paul reached into one of the kitchen cabinets and handed a small white box to Josephine. She hurried out the door. "My sweetie was an ER nurse for over forty years. She'll know what to do until the ambulance people take over."

"Both Leah and Shannon are worried about finding some missing mules. Do you know how many animals there should be?" Carlton and Paul walked closer to the barn.

"I think the count is around twenty at the moment. I wondered why it got quiet after they tied us up. Those critters usually keep up a pretty loud tune."

"Shannon said something about the crooks running off the mules." Carlton wondered how long it would take for the ambulance to arrive.

"I heard a lot of racket after those ornery men tied us up. It sounded like a stampede was going on. The mules should come back for supper, most of them anyway. We've had a few runaways." Paul chuckled.

Carlton flinched at the reminder of Sylvester's escape as the older man continued.

"There are a couple of back pastures they might be grazing while they kick up their heels. I can direct you there. I might even ride out with you if the Missus gives me permission. It's been a while since I got to roam around the old place." A wistful expression filled Paul's face

"It sounds like you've been here for a long time." Carlton raised his eyebrows as he studied the other man.

"Yup, we used to own the place before Miss Leah bought us out. Josephine said it was time to let someone younger take over the ranching. I raised cattle, but the mules sure liven up the place. I miss the country, but I'm getting pretty good at playing Rook at our senior condos' gathering place."

The piercing sound of an ambulance siren filled the air, ending their conversation. Help had arrived.

Chapter Fifteen

Leah sat by her forewoman until the emergency responders took over. Josephine had managed to keep Shannon awake, but she'd also urged caution about moving the patient. They'd piled more covers on top of the saddle blanket, keeping the injured woman warm. As the medics transferred her to the ambulance, she'd apologized for the mules running off.

"Don't worry. I'll get them rounded up before you get back here. It wasn't your fault. Someone's trying to get Sylvester back in their clutches." Leah's mind spun with what the men had done.

"They asked about him. I didn't tell them where he was," Shannon murmured.

"Praise the Lord." Leah squeezed Shannon's hand.

"I'm sorry they found out where your rescue ranch was. I know how you've always said to keep it a secret." Shannon's voice quivered.

"I know you've never betrayed me. I think they must have followed Kent and Winnie out here." At least that concept worked in theory. What about Penny and the overheard conversation? How had the henchmen known to follow Kent? She waved as the ambulance carried Shannon away from the ranch. Grabbing a discarded blanket and saddle, she headed for the mules in the corral. She noted that the horses she and Carlton had left tied at the edge of the forest had joined the three remaining mules. He must have brought them in while she sat with Shannon.

"Need some help?" Carlton grabbed another set of gear from her tack room and limped toward her, with Paul following close behind. They both carried the saddles especially made for mule riding.

"Sure. Let's take the mules. They know the territory better and aren't tired." As they saddled up, her mind raced. "How do you think the crooks knew to come here? Did you ask Kent and Winnie if anyone followed them?"

"I just checked with them. There was no sign of anyone on the road. They even circled around several times on the way here." He paused from cinching up the saddle. "My thoughts are with what Penny said when we listened in. I think we need to have the police bring her in for questioning."

"I won't argue with that." Betrayal from the woman who'd boosted her career sent a shard of anger to her gut as her thoughts swirled. The author's box... Penny had carried it to Carlton's vehicle. Someone busted a window in his house when the container was in his SUV. "Where is the box that Kent and Winnie brought here for me?"

"Let's see if they still have it."

They led their mules to where the Russells were staring at the open trunk of their car. The box of author paraphernalia lay on its side next to Leah's unopened suitcase. Bookmarks, pens, and notepads spilled out.

Kent held an arm out in front of Winnie. "Don't disturb anything. They wanted something from the box."

"We think it might have been a tracker since Carlton's house was vandalized when he had the box and then someone followed you here when the box was in your possession." Leah wanted to stomp her foot, but didn't want the mule she led to shy away. Instead, she leaned into the animal's face and rubbed its neck.

"If there was a tracker, the evidence is gone. They were looking for something, based on the mess. I wondered why they took my keys and then left them here in the trunk." Kent pulled a notepad from his pocket and wrote a few notes while Carlton dialed 911 again.

After a brief conversation, he turned to the others. "A deputy should be here soon. They didn't come with the ambulance because of an accident. Several officers are still on the scene."

"I hope everyone is okay." Leah laid a hand on her chest. "Will Shannon's ambulance have to stop there on the way to the hospital?"

"No one needed an ambulance at the wreck. Shannon should reach the hospital in a few minutes. The incident was on another road, running near the eastern side of your property. There was a hit and run. Before they had time to respond, the victim disconnected her phone and fled the scene on foot. The deputies suggested we not go after the missing mules until they round up their runner and the other driver."

"A person on foot won't get far if they are heading this way. I've got tall fences on that side of the property. My mules need to come home and I'm going after them. Some of my herd has abuse issues. They may think I abandoned them like their former owners." Leah led Marty Mule over to two concrete steps to mount him. He and the other two mules in the corral were some of her oldest acquisitions, and she didn't want to push them too hard, but the younger animals were on the run. There was no other choice. "We'll go slowly for these older mules. If we can't find the others in an hour we can head back and let the law take care of their runner." She leaned over Marty's shoulder. "Let's do this, old boy."

As she left the yard, she looked back in time to see Kent hand Carlton a knife and a gun belt. Paul had already fallen in behind her. She was surprised Josephine had let her husband go so easily, but the grin on his face reflected his excitement at riding again. Swift moving hooves indicated Carlton was catching up with them.

"Smooth ride. I'm not bouncing like when I'm on a horse." Carlton's smile warmed her thoughts.

"I told you mules were better." She couldn't stop the pride rising in her chest.

"We'll see how long they last on this chase of ours." Carlton matched her pace as she pushed Marty ahead.

"Longer than a horse would. Mules provide endurance rides, even these old guys. This is Marty, by the way. He's still my favorite."

"The comic strip hero?" Carlton's gaze roamed across the mule and then met her look.

"The one and only." She leaned forward and gave the old mule's neck a pat

"Should we check the west pasture first?" Paul interrupted as he took the lead.

"Let's go east. We'll clear it first to avoid meeting up with the deputy's runner." Leah let the older man lead, figuring he was enjoying the ride. They rode in silence until reaching an open field. A few heads bobbed up when they approached. Marty brayed long and loud. The others answered. It looked like over half her herd had found the field full of dried grass.

Leah stuck two fingers in her mouth and whistled. Most of the mules meandered in her direction. Paul and Carlton began circling and herding the mules toward the trail they'd arrived on. Two youngsters bellowed and brayed as their heads pushed against the tall fence marking her boundary line. Leah headed in their direction.

She muttered, "Stubborn mules," glad that Carlton was out of hearing distance. She needed to increase the new arrivals' training. Her breath clogged her throat. She stared at a woman's body, clad in bright yellow, lying against the fence across from where the two colts brayed.

~~~~~

Carlton paused as the mules in front of him shifted to head back to the pasture. A faint whistle reached his ears. He turned and saw Leah frantically waving her arms as she sat on Marty the Mule. When he lifted his hand in recognition, she quit whistling and beckoned for him to come closer.

"Hey, Paul, head these mules back to the ranch. I'm going to see what's bothering Leah."

Paul swung behind the ones Carlton had been trailing and headed them toward the barn as he approached Leah.
~~~~~

"Is something wrong with those two creatures?" Carlton eyed the two mules making strange noises.

She shook her head and pointed mutely at the body lying just outside the fence. Leah's face was pale, a contrast to the normal tan he'd come to appreciate. As he studied the twisted body, he recognized Penny's pantsuit. The outfit now had rips and blood splatters, but he could tell it was the same bright yellow outfit the agent had worn when taking them out to eat.

"Is she dead?" Leah's voice shook.

Carlton dismounted and reached through the fence with two fingers. Warmth and slight movement met his touch. "She's alive for now." He checked his phone. Only a single dot remained for a connection. He opted for a text to Kent. *Found Penny, barely alive. Send the lawmen to eastern fence. She needs medics.*

Leah knelt close to the fence and reached in Penny's direction. "Come on, Penny. You need to live. I forgive you. God can too."

He shook his head in disbelief. Forgiving someone like Penny took a better spirit than his. The agent deserved any pain she felt for her betrayal of the author she was supposed to be supporting.

"Keep breathing, Penny. I'm here for you." Leah's fingers rubbed against Penny's side.

A faint whisper came from Penny. "Sorry. The men...I had to do it for her... She..." The agent's head slumped to the side.

"Penny?" Leah's fingers reached through the fence.

"Is she still breathing?" Carlton wasn't sure he wanted to know. Emotions vied in his chest about comforting Leah or rejoicing that they were through with the woman's betrayal.

"Yes." Leah sighed. She leaned against the fence and closed her eyes.

Carlton figured she was praying. He chose to focus on Penny's last words. The men were still going to be coming after them. Getting Leah to safety had to be a priority.

Now that his car and the tracking devices were missing, maybe Carlton could find a safe place to hide Leah. He wondered about going to his sister's therapy ranch. Was it too close to Leah's own place? That might make the author happier, but he wasn't sure about the proximity. They had leaked too much information to Penny about Tamera's place. Was he even capable of keeping Leah safe? He looked at the mule standing next to him. Getting off to check Penny's status had been a mistake. He couldn't even get in the saddle unless someone came to boost him up.

A sound from the distance made him place a hand on the gun Kent had given him. "Who's there?"

"I'm Deputy Morris, along with the K-9 officer from Forest Glen. Officer Marta Miller and her dog helped track our missing driver to this spot. We have some medical techs too. Your boss called and mentioned the need for emergency services."

Carlton's shoulders relaxed as he welcomed the arrival of help.

They watched helplessly as Penny was loaded onto a stretcher. Carlton spoke for Leah and himself as he explained what they knew.

The deputy nodded in appreciation. "Let us know if you need our help again. We can send a patrol car by the property several times today if that will help."

"Thanks. That would be great. We'll keep in touch." Carlton watched the law personnel and medics disappear into the trees before turning to stare at his ride. He had another mountain to conquer, or it would take all day to get back to the barn.

"Have you ever mounted from the wrong side?" Leah reached up and climbed onto Marty from the right side of the animal's torso. "I've trained my older mules to accept a rider from the left or right. Miss Jenny Lou won't give you any problems if you want to give it a try."

His eyebrows rose in disbelief. Such a simple solution, but would it work? "None of Tamera's horses would allow a right-side mount."

"That's because they haven't been trained. I like to teach my mules balance." Leah guided Marty closer to Carlton's female ride and reached a hand across the saddle from the left. "I'll be here to help."

Carlton held her hand as he bounced several times. Her strength surprised him as he rose and flung his weak leg across the back of the female mule. The jenny stood still, but she released a wheezing bray. Carlton's chest tightened with a quick breath of his own. Leah's hand belonged in his. The thought whirled through his heart.

Leah released his hand and backed her ride away. He missed the contact as thoughts of protecting her filled the vacuum.

"Let's go get the rest of my herd. I don't want to worry about them wandering around." She abruptly headed down the trail, herding the two younger mules, who'd located Penny, in front.

"Don't you think we should go back to the ranch?" He couldn't believe she still wanted to find the wandering animals that were enjoying grazing in the pastures.

"There were only a few missing. It wouldn't surprise me if Paul already has them rounded up and will meet us on the trail."

For her sake, Carlton hoped she was right.

Chapter Sixteen

Leah's shoulders fell as tension rolled away. The missing mules plodded toward her along a worn path heading from the western pasture toward the barn. Winnie and Kent had joined Paul as they herded the group of mules forward. In the back of her mind, she remembered Winnie mentioning being a rider. That fact had slipped Leah's mind during the upsetting events of the last few days. The older woman's herding ability on the mule overshadowed her husband's, as he tried to keep a straying mule headed in the right direction. Leah couldn't help but chuckle.

"Are you laughing at my boss's expense?" Carlton pulled up next to her as they both guided their mounts off the trail to let the others pass by.

"Yup. I don't think he's done much wrangling." She held Marty back as he attempted to shove forward into the line of moving mules.

"Kent only wrangles people most of the time. He's great at getting what he wants from two-legged creatures. Winnie is the only one that gives him much trouble."

"They're a great couple. What are you talking about?" Leah adored the pair who'd become her online friends after Sylvester's escapades. Having a fellow writer and illustrator deepened the relationship. Hiring Kent's business for protection had been an added blessing, though she'd struggled at first when a lame man had shown up. She knew better now. Carlton was a brave and intelligent man who'd protected her despite his limp. She'd decided she didn't mind one bit that he was handsome and humble.

Carlton's voice infiltrated her thoughts. "Kent and Winnie dated back when they were young, until she left without a word."

"I knew they were newlyweds, but I did not know they had a history." Curiosity grew as she nudged Marty back on the trail to the ranch.

Jenny Lou followed with Carlton, who pulled abreast to speak. "Her boss at work was a criminal and told Winnie if her lawman boyfriend got news of what the company was up to, Kent would be a dead man. She left them both and hid for years."

"That was a bold move, but sad at the same time." Leah had done her share of hiding so she understood some of Winnie's motivation.

Carlton nodded. "Our last federal case involved taking down the business for good and finding Winnie, who served as a key witness. By that time, Kent was a widower with grandkids who adored Winnie Gee books. In the end, Kent and Winnie overcame the past and married."

"Kent must be a very forgiving man." Leah dared to bring up the topic of forgiveness.

"He was and is. He's forgiven me for mistakes I've made, like having someone in my care kidnapped. I find it harder to forgive myself." Carlton frowned and looked off in the distance.

"Is that why you were uncomfortable during the preacher's sermon on forgiveness this morning?" Probing wasn't a good idea, but she did it anyway, wanting to know more about the man riding next to her.

"You didn't look at ease yourself. Maybe you need to forgive someone too." Carlton pushed Jenny Lou forward, leaving Leah to deal with her own thoughts.

He was right. She wasn't perfect either. Trying to forgive her kidnapper only worked to a point. Forgetting the memories and the ensuing lifestyle changes were another thing. Did she need to seek forgiveness from her father for denying him joy in the family heritage? She squirmed in her seat, earning a bray from Marty. She faced ahead and pushed her mule to catch up and then pass the others. Her issues with forgiveness were problems for another day.

Right now, the focus should be on Sylvester. The need to call the veterinarian pressed hard into her conscience. She should make sure things were still fine at his clinic. Had the enemy figured out where the mule was? The number of clinics working with large animals was limited. But she'd never indicated he was ill, unless that was something the enemy anticipated.

When she arrived back at the ranch, she noticed Carlton's sister was closing the door to her horse trailer. Tamera must have arrived to take the borrowed horses back to their home.

Leah rode closer. "May I borrow your phone? I need to check with my vet and see how one of my mules is doing. I don't want to take the chance that my phone is bugged."

"No problem." Tamera passed the phone and stepped away to help her brother open the corral gates wide for the last mules being herded in.

As the phone rang, Leah counted the animals and was relieved to see that all were now in the pen. Their complaining brays made it difficult to hear when someone finally answered her call. "Hold on a second, I need to move away from some noisy critters."

"Yes, ma'am."

She barely caught the person's reply as she moved away from the corral. "Can you hear me better now?"

"I sure can. Is this the mule lady? You must be checking on Sylvester." The youthful voice sounded like a teen or college intern. Doc often had volunteers helping with the animals.

"That would be me. How is he doing?" Leah chewed her lip as she waited for an answer.

"He's recovering just fine. We tried to call you earlier but didn't get an answer."

"Sorry, I've had my cell off recently. Did you say Sylvester is recovering?"

"Yeah, his infection finally went down enough for Doc to work on him. The operation was a success. That mule is a strong one and he's doing fine except for being ornery."

"That's great." She breathed a silent prayer of thanks to God. "Has anyone been asking about Sylvester besides me?"

"No, but Doc had some questions about what he found. Can you come in as soon as possible? Your mule and my boss both need someone to calm them down."

"Sure. I'll be there soon." A faint bray in the background reassured Leah of Sylvester's presence as she hit the button disconnecting the call.

She led Marty to his stall, removed his tack, and after cleaning his hooves, brushed him down. "Good boy." He pushed at her with his nose. "I'll have to find a treat for you later."

"Here, Paul gave me plenty." Carlton held out a handful of treats as he leaned over the stall door. "I already gave Jenny Lou her share." His voice was friendly. She was relieved that he'd apparently moved on from their conversation about forgiveness.

"Thanks. Now, we need to find a ride to my vet's place. Sylvester had his operation and the doctor wants to share what he removed from him."

"I'll see about borrowing Tamera's truck. She's been outside waiting to see if we need her help. If you want to pick up Sylvester while we're there, we can bring her trailer, too, once we drop off Jim's horses."

"That should work. The park where we got on the horses isn't far from the vet's. Let's get going. I'm anxious to see my mule before any other disasters happen." Leah left Marty's stall and headed out of the barn.

Carlton's cane thumped behind her. "Speaking of disasters, we might want to leave Jim's horses at Tamera's place for now. Whoever is watching us may have their eyes on Jim too."

<p style="text-align:center">~~~~~</p>

Carlton waved his sister aside as he pulled himself into the driver's seat. "We're going to hope no one follows us, but if they do, I've been trained to deal with difficult driving scenarios."

"Sure, boss," Tamera teased as she slid to the middle seat. He'd have much preferred to have Leah rubbing elbows with him like before, but it was better that he wouldn't be distracted.

After Leah climbed into the passenger seat, he drove the rig down the rescue ranch's lane and onto the road running in front of both properties. He checked his side mirrors looking for followers. None appeared. Two minutes later they pulled into the drive for Tamera's horse therapy ranch and parked near her barn.

The red barn still looked in good shape, though Tamera might want to touch up a couple of places where the paint was peeling. If his leg hadn't been in bad shape, he should have done a few things during his recovery. Maybe he could offer to hire someone to paint the structure.

He'd spent many hours working with horses and hiding in the old barn when the ranch had been a place to rescue lonely boys. Tamera only had four horses of her own, but there were boarders that took up a few other stalls. The rental income helped his sister run the place and keep her out of the red. There would still be room for Jim's two mounts, until they could arrange to get them home.

"You stay put. We'll get the horses out quickly." Tamera slid away to follow Leah, who'd already headed for the trailer's back gate. He didn't know whether to feel relieved or embarrassed. They were right about removing the animals faster than he could. Limitations were hard to get used to. He watched them lead the horses into the barn.

Seconds later, Leah was back in the truck with a determined expression on her face. "Tamera's taking care of both horses. Let's get going. The vet's assistant suggested we hurry."

"What's going on with your mule?" he asked as he maneuvered back to the road.

"Sylvester isn't happy about being cut on and the veterinarian wants to talk about what he found."

"Show me where to go." He paused at stop sign until she directed him to proceed straight east.

She pulled her phone from her pocket and held it out. "I can use the GPS on my phone if you want me to turn it on."

He shook his head. "That might not be the best idea since we never determined if your phone was tracked. Give me an idea of where we're headed and we'll start with that."

"The Mill Stream Large Animal Service is the vet I use." She sat back in her seat and tugged at her seatbelt strap, loosening it up as she leaned to put her phone away.

"They're the same vet Tamera uses. I can get there without relying on either of our phones, but I might go around the block a few times in case someone has eyes on us." Carlton ran several scenarios through his mind for traveling there.

"Good idea. I know I can trust you." The strength in her voice gave him confidence.

Her trust meant a lot. She'd doubted him at the convention. That had been obvious. Now he needed to live up to that trust. Checking his mirrors again, he noticed a vehicle following them at a distance. He took a turn and went around three quarters of the mile square before returning to the direct route they'd been on before. Sure enough the vehicle followed them, but stayed far back.

"It looks like we have company. They don't seem to want to play bumper car yet, but they're intent on following us." He checked his side mirror again.

"What should we do?"

"We'll keep driving for now. There's another vet Tamera uses when the Mill Stream doctor isn't available. We're going to go about twenty miles out of the way and see if they follow us to the other vet. That place is close enough to the city that I think it's in the jurisdiction that my old friend Mark Wakefield serves as a policeman. His contact should be in my phone under recent calls. See if he can be on the lookout."

Leah made the call and put it on speaker after it started ringing.

"Hey, Cowboy. How are you? I figured it would be a while before I heard from you." Mark's voice rang with surprise.

"Well, I... Make that we could use your help. I'm still on bodyguard duty with Mara Shore, also known as Leach Beach. We've got a tail following us in a dark sedan, and plan to make a stop at Trotter's Equine Service in about half an hour. If that vet is in your jurisdiction, is there any way you can be there when we arrive?"

"I'll do my best as long as an emergency doesn't arise. I'm about fifteen minutes out." Radio squawking came through Mark's phone connection.

"Great. If you're in a squad car, maybe park out of sight?" Carlton passed a slow moving vehicle, noting that the sedan did the same a few seconds later.

"Will do. I'll check in at police headquarters and let them know what I'm doing."

"Thanks, buddy." Carlton knew he could count on Mark, even though they hadn't had recent contact.

"Leah Beach? Wasn't that the name of the rich girl that got

kidnapped when we were growing up?" Carlton watched Leah cringe as he took his gaze from the road for a split second.

"Yeah, but she doesn't want people knowing her real name. She's happy going by Mara Shore, the author, but you can keep that under your lid. She's listening right now and I know she'd appreciate you keeping the information to yourself."

"Mum's the word. I'll do my best to stake out the place before you arrive. I'm getting off to connect with my captain. If you don't hear anything, assume I'll be there." Mark ended the call.

Leah leaned back in her seat and clasped her hands. "Thanks, Carlton. I don't like reminders about the kidnapping. It took a long time to get over the betrayal."

"Are you sure you're over it now? You don't like being in public. You use a pen name. I'm glad you're getting more comfortable with the Russells and me, but even going to church seemed to make you uncomfortable."

As he spoke, her arms crossed her chest. She looked away without replying.

He concentrated on watching the road and their follower. He could only do so much, but he had people he wasn't afraid to call on. He picked up his phone from where she'd laid it on the dash and using a voice command, made the connection to let Kent know their plans.

Chapter Seventeen

Leah closed her eyes. Her blood boiled. Who was he to criticize her for being uncomfortable in church? He seemed more rattled than her when he dragged her from the worship service. What did he know about being a kidnap victim? Sure, he'd been there on the outside when the crooks kidnapped the girl in his custody. Carlton probably gave the child as much sympathy as her dad had years ago. At least she had her mules and the few people she trusted to look after them.

The word *mule* infiltrated her twisting thoughts as Carlton made another call on speaker phone. "Hey, Kent, we're doing a diversionary run to a different veterinary service called Trotter's Equine. It's near the city. I've got a tail following me. They seem content to keep their distance."

"Do you need me to head that way? We're almost back to Forest Glen. I'll drop Winnie off and meet you."

"We're good. A police friend of mine will meet us there and help apprehend if needed. Did you send anyone to the real vet where Sylvester is located?"

"Cara promised to go there right after church this morning. I haven't heard from her since. Let me give her a call and get back to you."

Leah forced herself to breathe while she waited for Kent to call back. She opened her eyes and watched the dashboard clock move at a snail's pace. When the phone rang again, she reached for it before Carlton could and put it on speaker.

"How is Sylvester?"

"He's fine. Cara is amused by his antics." Kent chuckled.

"Good. I was worried when you didn't call back right away." Relief poured over Leah as falling tension allowed her shoulders to relax.

"I contacted a friend, Artie, who works at the hospital. I let him know Penny is part of a case we're working on. He was glad I called. The ER doctor wants to contact her family for permission to proceed. Do you have anything I can share?" Kent asked.

"She was a private person when it came to personal information. She did mention having sick parents that had concerned her over the last few months. The burden of helping them was the excuse she used for her recent money-hungry attitude. That's all I know, other than she worked through a group in Chicago, before going independent within the last year. I think that's when her attitude started changing." Leah wished she had more information, but Penny had always been business focused.

"Okay. I'll reach out to the local federal office tomorrow and see if they can run a check on Penny. We may need their full involvement if this case gets any messier. My former secretary and her new boss will be in after 8:30 tomorrow morning."

"What about getting Penny the help she needs?" As angry as Leah had been at her agent's betrayal, she didn't want the woman to die in the hospital. No one deserved that, especially one who didn't exhibit a belief in God.

"I'll let the hospital know we don't have any contacts. They'll proceed as best they can with emergency care. They are required to help her." Kent's voice soothed Leah's worries as she offered a silent prayer for Penny's recovery.

After slowing for an intersection, Carlton answered. "Thanks for the update. Let Cara know the animal hospital is in the crosshairs of at least a couple of dangerous men."

"I'll do that. You two watch yourselves. We don't know who we're dealing with, other than they are desperate. Give me a call after you confront your follower at Trotter's." Two beeps from Carlton's phone indicated Kent had ended the call.

Carlton tapped his fingers on the steering wheel. "Are you ready to talk about our arrival at Trotter's?"

"Sure. How do you plan to handle that?" She jutted out her chin, determined to do her part.

"We'll go inside and then see what happens. I want you to go first while I watch for trouble. I'll come after you're safely inside. We'll need to warn the people in the clinic, though hopefully Mark has taken care of telling them what is going on before we arrive. If the crooks come toward the building bearing weapons, I'm sure Mark and the police will take over. We won't be alone. I'm thankful for those who are helping us."

Leah nodded. The temptation to think his comment about helpers was a dig at her loner lifestyle was tempting, but the prayer she'd offered for Penny had infiltrated her wayward thoughts. "I'll pray and do my best to stay safe. I'm glad you have friends who are willing to help. I may not have companions like yours, but I have God." The longer she thought on things, attending church that morning hadn't been as scary as she'd feared it would be. "Maybe in the future, I can make some acquaintances at church too."

Carlton cleared his throat. "Yeah, I had hoped to ease into the idea without hearing a lesson on forgiveness on my first day back in a while."

He reached out a hand and she accepted it with a squeeze. He released her hand when he put on a turn signal a little bit later. "We're here. Are you ready?"

She nodded and released her seatbelt as he came to a stop in front of a building with a western facade. Neighing came from the pole barn behind the office. He'd parked close enough that it was only a few steps to the open office door. Once she stepped inside the building's vacated waiting room, she noticed a police woman waving from a room down a side hall. Leah headed toward the officer with Carlton right behind.

They stayed hidden in an exam room for several minutes as they waited. And waited.

Mark's voice coming over the policewoman's radio finally broke the silence. "I'm coming in the building. No need to hide."

He frowned as he came through a back door, shaking his head. "Either they made us or decided to watch and wait somewhere until later. A couple of dark sedans drove by, but without any other identifiers, I couldn't justify a chase. Traffic here is thick and moving in waves. It was hard to tell if people were checking out the place or just caught in the ebb and flow."

Carlton shook Mark's hand. "Thanks for trying. Do we need to hang around and see if anyone shows up later?"

"Maybe tie your trailer door in an open position so they can see you didn't pick up your mule here. Head back to the safety of your home. We'll keep the vet and his staff safe and provide a police presence through the night to see if anyone shows up."

Mark's suggestion sounded like a good idea for their travels, but Leah didn't want to risk other animals being harmed.

"What about the barn residents?" Leah remembered the horse's whinny from earlier.

"The vet says there's only one boarded horse back there and his owner, who was on a weekend vacation, is showing up within the hour to take him home." The policewoman smiled for the first time. "My car is behind the barn. When I parked, I think the horse thought I'd come to set him free."

"I just wish we could be free from our troublemakers." Leah nodded her thanks before trudging back to the truck to help Carlton secure the trailer door in an open position.

~~~~~

Carlton's phone rang as he climbed into the driver's seat. The caller ID indicated law enforcement. "Hello."

"Is this Carlton Marsh who recently reported a missing SUV?"

"I am. Have you found my vehicle?" Hope stirred in his chest.
~~~~~

"We have it here at the Forest Glen police station. You can come and claim it any time."

"Can you tell me where my SUV was found?" Carlton put the phone on speaker so he could get the truck started. Leah smiled at him and gave a thumbs up.

They could hear papers rattle as the officer answered. "Our tow truck pulled it in from one of our downtown neighborhoods. The homeowners called because the bumper blocked their driveway."

"Is there any damage to the car?" Carlton put the truck in gear and started moving to the edge of the vet's parking lot.

"There are a few scratches on the bumper, but you mentioned those when you reported the missing vehicle. We'd like you to look over your car for other damage before we release it."

"I'm on my way as soon as I check on one thing. Thank you." He disconnected the phone and turned to Leah as he waited for traffic to clear. "Would you be comfortable driving my SUV back to Tamera's place from Forest Glen?"

"That won't be a problem. I can drive either vehicle if you want. I've hauled a trailer of mules before."

"You'll be safer in the SUV if you need to escape from our troublemakers. It's my job to be your guard and having you in the more maneuverable vehicle would be the best choice. Being in two vehicles isn't ideal but would be efficient."

"I hope the crooks fall into your friend's trap, here at Trotter's."

"That would be great, but there are no guarantees they will come back to this vet's place." Carlton turned the vehicle south toward Forest Glen.

"Speaking of vets, I still need to check on Sylvester. The vet's assistant said Doc wanted to ask me something about what he removed during the operation." Leah switched her visor to the side of the truck's window as the sun sank lower in the west.

He lifted a hand above his eyes as bright rays filled the gap on the windshield. "Use my phone and see if the information can wait until morning or he can tell you over the phone. If that doesn't work, ask Sylvester's doctor to tell Cara, since she's there for the mule's protection." He chuckled. "I'll have to tease her about being a mule's bodyguard." He figured Cara would think he was funny.

"Don't laugh at her expense. I've been a mule bodyguard for a long time. Someone has to stick up for their rights."

"Pardon me, I beg for your forgiveness." Carlton cringed after bringing up the subject that had silenced them earlier.

"So, we're back to forgiveness."

"Make a call to your vet. Maybe I'll tell you more details about what I need to forgive, if you share yours."

"You already kind of know." She didn't sound like she wanted to continue the conversation any more than he did, but he thought sharing might help clear the tension between them.

"We've got plenty of time for details." He did want to understand and know her better.

"Fine. Let me have your phone, so I can call Dr. Sanders."

"Help yourself." He pointed to where it lay on the dash. He heard the phone ring for a long time, and no one answered.

"Do you have Cara's number?" Concern laced her voice.

"Yeah." Carlton gave the voice command to call Kent's female employee.

"Hey, Carlton. What's up?" Cara answered after the second ring.

"We tried calling the vet and no one answered. Is everything okay?" He was relieved to hear her answer the phone.

"They called it a night. The vet and his assistant were only here to take care of Sylvester because it's a Sunday. Since I'm an experienced horsewoman and currently a mule bodyguard, they laughed and left me alone with this braying beast." Sylvester's complaints came through Cara's end of the conversation.

"Did the vet say anything about what he took out of Sylvester?" Leah asked.

"He showed it to me. I suggested he drop it with the sheriff's office when he left, but he said something about taking it to a chemistry professor at the college in the morning before coming back. The thing was seeping some kind of fluid into Sylvester's system. Dr. Sanders said Sylvester should be a healthier and less irritating mule without the implant."

"That's good to hear. Have a good night guarding Sylvester. We'll stop by tomorrow if all goes well." Carlton hung up the phone and returned to concentrating on the road.

"You go first." Leah's voice broke the silence.

"Huh?" What was she asking?

"Tell me the details about your struggle with forgiveness."

Chapter Eighteen

Carlton gripped the steering wheel. Divulging the double hit from life that had taken so much from him wasn't something he wanted to do. But if talking about the past would heal his relationship with God and other people, he decided to give it a chance. "How far back should I go?"

"Starting from the beginning would be fine."

Okay. He could work up to the things bothering him right now. "After I got over my mom dying, my life goal, other than riding horses, involved working in law enforcement. The man who acted as our father at the ranch had been a policeman until he decided preventing boys from taking up lives of crime seemed more important than stopping criminals."

"He sounds like a smart man." Leah's comment confirmed what he'd always believed about the man who'd been his hero.

Contentment washed over Carlton as he recalled his mentor. "Pa Dudley and his wife had no children of their own. When his parents passed away, they left him the land and a few horses. Pa took early retirement, and he returned to the home he'd grown up in. Between income from fostering kids, running a farm, and Ma's salary as a teacher, they supported a family of boys. Some came to stay forever, like me, while others came and went as their family situations changed. Pa kept us busy and on task like we were a troop of his former police recruits. It was no surprise that several of us went into law enforcement. Mark and I are just a sample of those that did."

"I'm sure both of you made him proud." The setting sun burnished Leah's dark hair with reddish highlights.

Carlton looked away from the beautiful woman and focused on the farmland lining the road and his past. "After Mark and I went to the police academy together, I chose to continue training to prepare for the federal agency. A couple of years later, I returned to Ohio for a position in Kent's division. It was nice to be near the sister that I'd gotten to know during my last year or so at the Dudley's ranch. Tamera had become their cook and manager. Her life was secure after Ma and Pa Dudley gave her a family loan to buy the property and turn it into the therapy ranch. My career was on track as a federal agent. I enjoyed being involved in the church. Asking my girlfriend to marry me was the next step toward fulfillment."

"You had an ideal life. My life has been more solitary." Leah sighed.

He chanced a look her way. Pensive best described her expression. She had it better than he did, but probably didn't realize it. "I might be envious of your solitude. You avoided the suffering I endured when everything went downhill during my stint as a federal agent. My first injury came during a stake-out taking down a major group of criminals. They shot my upper leg from under me.

"Due to complications with an infection, I lost my ability to give my fiancée the very thing she wanted, the chance to have children of her own. The doctor said odds were against me fathering children. Once she understood we probably wouldn't have children of our own, she called off the wedding. I guess I should be grateful for that, but it still hurt. She wouldn't consider adoption."

"That's terrible. I'm estranged from my adopted father at the moment, but he and mom took me into their home and raised me from the time I was a baby. I miss seeing him."

"Unfortunately, I still see my ex around town. She attends the church we went to this morning, which is one of the reasons I wasn't happy about going." He didn't feel inclined to share that he'd seen his former fiancée that morning.

"Have you thought about attending a different church?" Leah looked away.

"Tamera goes to the small congregation the Dudleys went to when they ran the ranch. She's asked me to come, but I haven't been ready to consider going."

"Maybe going to a smaller place of worship would feel more comfortable. I think it would for me." She nodded and seemed to be reflecting on her thoughts or just watching the flat land along the road.

"I have a lot to be forgiven. I'm not sure I'd even feel welcome in a small congregation. During my recovery at Tamera's place, criminals kidnapped a girl I was responsible for. I failed her and the agency. Then that mule of yours reinjured my leg, making a full recovery impossible." He fisted his right hand on the seat beside him.

She placed her palm over his tight fingers. "I wish I'd known about Sylvester injuring you at that time. I've tried to let you know how sorry I am."

"Yeah, I heard you before. It's my problem. I feel unable to deal with forgiving myself and the ones that caused all my difficulties. Are you happy knowing all that?" He regretted the harsh tone in his voice. Instead of apologizing he chose not to comment further as he withdrew the hand she held and placed it back on the steering wheel.

She leaned away. "I appreciate you sharing. Knowing where you're coming from helps me understand you better."

Carlton turned on the older model truck's headlights as the sky darkened. He hoped she couldn't see the frown he felt creasing his forehead. "Now it's your turn to share."

For a moment the truck cab remained silent. Then, she cleared her throat. "I know what it's like to be the kidnapped girl. That event changed my whole way of dealing with people. Forgiving a boyfriend who was supposed to love me enough to have a close relationship is something I've never gotten over. I don't trust people like I should.

"I blame my father's fame for making the guy use me for his own motives. Dad and I have never been as close as we should have been. I think he wanted natural children of his own like your former girlfriend. After the kidnapping, we lost what little connection we had. I've avoided people most of my life."

"That's pretty obvious, based on what I've seen in the last couple of days, including this morning." Carlton braked as a deer ran in front of the truck. He scanned the sides of the road for any herd members following their leader, before getting back up to speed.

Leah removed her hand from the dash where she'd placed it when he slowed. "I was scared to attend the worship service today but realize how much I've missed out on by not having others to worship with." Her voice trembled. He couldn't tell if it was from their conversation or nearly slamming the deer.

"So, do you think you'll start attending church after this morning?" Carlton watched a car closing in. Relief filled him when the sports car whipped past the slower moving truck and headed down the road without bothering them.

"I'm giving church attendance some thought, but maybe the events of the last few days taught me that I am doing the right thing by hiding from the strangers who only want to harm me and my animals."

"You still sound hurt." Carlton shoved his own hurts to the side as he tried to concentrate on her difficulties.

"I know that feeling too well. The abused mules I've adopted come to me hurt and angry. I want to lash out at their owners, but I don't have enough courage. I do have the ability to help the animals get over the past. The comic strip and the graphic novel have given me an outlet to express my feelings and their needs in a humorous way. Maybe both of us need a way to get over our hurts."

"So, do you have a plan in mind for us?" Carlton wasn't a planner. He was an action kind of guy and following some long list wasn't his way.

"The only thing that works for my mules is tons of patience to win them over with one small step at a time."

"Old habits are hard to break." Especially when dealing with a new handicap.

"I know." Her reply was so soft, he barely heard it.

"Ma Dudley always said when it came to teaching a lesson that was too hard, the best thing was to break everything into small concepts and then use that to understand the next thing. I learned a lot about dealing with other people from her."

"She sounds like a wise woman."

Carlton smiled at the memories of the gracious woman who'd been more of a mother than his own. "I still miss her good advice. I sometimes wonder if I should have been a teacher like her instead of law enforcement. I didn't always listen to her advice since I wanted things to come together fast. I guess that's why I chose the police academy instead of college. I'd give anything to have a good talk with her today."

"Are the Dudleys still around?"

"They moved to a retirement village after leaving the ranch. Ma's thinking ability faded too soon. She and Pa arranged for Tamera to take over the ranch after Ma's health began to fail. Knowing that my sister would be using horses to help people heal or deal with life's frustrations made Ma and Pa Dudley happy. They deeded the place over to her and forgave the rest of the loan when it looked like the end of their lives was near. They passed away about a year ago, within a month of each other."

"Helping mules heal helps me too."

"You should see if Tamera might add a few mules to her therapy program." He was sure his sister would be interested. She'd mentioned the possibility before, but her neighbor's reclusive ways hadn't offered the opportunity for a discussion.

She turned toward him, excitement bubbling in her voice. "I might have a couple of male mules ready for giving rides to those who need a gentle ride for therapy." She leaned back against her seat. "Are we avoiding solving our problems?"

"Probably." Carlton had welcomed a diversion.

"How about prayer? I pray all the time. God hears me despite my running away from the world."

She was back to curing him of his problems.

"I pray when I'm desperate. I just don't feel the closeness I had when growing up on the Dudley farm." He wasn't a total heathen, was he?

"Being close to the Lord takes work. God wants to hear your voice." She wasn't giving up.

"He likes having you gather with others in worship too." Carlton decided a comeback was fair play.

"Touché. You're right. Something deep inside did feel a pull to worship with others during the service today. I loved singing with the group." She sighed. "I've survived a book tour and a comic convention. I'll give going to church on Sunday a challenge to overcome. How about you? Are you willing to forgive God and all the others who've wounded you?"

"I'll try. That's all I can promise." Carlton pulled into the Forest Glen Police Station parking lot and turned off the engine as his thoughts kept churning.

~~~~~

Leah watched Carlton get out of the vehicle. If a man with a limp could stomp, he was putting feet and cane into that action. She said a prayer of her own for strength and a safe drive to Tamera's home, as she watched him enter the station and return moments later with an officer. The two men approached Carlton's SUV where it sat under a streetlight and then they circled the vehicle. A light from Carlton's cell lit the darkness as they continued their inspection of the exterior. The officer bent low and she presumed they were looking for tracking devices. She was tired of trackers and appreciated the effort. Then a kick of guilt crossed her mind.

I'm doing it again. By staying in the car and letting Carlton talk to the cop, I'm avoiding people. Help me, Lord, to go over and ... socialize.

She pushed open the door and headed over to where the two men were shaking hands. "Hi, I'm Leah. Did everything check out?"

"The vehicle looks clean. Carlton says the scratches were there from a recent fender bender. I'm Officer Perlman." He extended his hand as an overly friendly expression crossed his face. Leah managed a quick handshake before stepping closer to her bodyguard. No one had flirted with her since...

"Are you ready for me to drive?" She made a point of focusing on Carlton, who laid a protective arm across her shoulders.

"Sure." His voice scratched like a voice-changing teen's. "Here's the key. I'll see you back at the ranch." He held open the door to his SUV for Leah to climb in.

"Take care, you two." The officer waved goodbye with a chuckle. "Nice meeting you both."

Carlton leaned in and held her hand for a moment. "I'll be on your six, doing my best to guard you safely to Tamera's. Give me a second to get buckled into the truck."

Leah nodded. She needed the time alone to think through the events of the last few minutes. Had she just flirted with Carlton? She might have, but she was rusty at best. His warm hand touching hers
~~~~~

moments ago had given her a thrill she hadn't dared to explore in years.

Breaking that barrier felt good, exciting, and full of possibilities. She started the SUV. Carlton blinked his headlights. She headed out into the moonlit countryside, and he followed. In some ways it felt good to be alone with her thoughts after a few days of constant supervision by a bodyguard. In other ways, she missed being next to Carlton. He was growing on her.

The ride went smoothly as they left Forest Glen and headed west. His presence behind her filled her with comfort. Her heart sank when he started flashing his high beams and signaling a right turn. They were nowhere near their destination. What had gone wrong now? She slowed and turned off at the next parking area near a diner. He pulled the truck in next to her and rolled down the passenger window.

"Is everything all right?" She couldn't keep the panic out of her voice as she opened her own window.

"My stomach was growling. It's been a long time since we ate with Penny for lunch. Charley Burgers is the place that Winnie and Kent like to eat."

"I'm hungry too. Let's go in, if you think it's safe." Leah sniffed. Scents from fried comfort food wafted in the air.

"We're good. I eat here often and would recognize any troublemakers the minute they came in the door. Mark called me a few minutes ago. I'd like to update you."

"Is everything okay?" She placed a hand on her fluttering chest.

"Things are better. I'll tell you more after we place our order. I'm starved." Carlton rolled the truck window up and got out. Leah did the same.

Charley Burgers had several customers. A jukebox played a country song in the background as they entered. After walking to the counter, they placed an order at the counter for two Charley Burgers with crinkle fries and two apple turnovers. The gum-chewing gal behind the counter gave them their drinks and a call number to set on their table. They claimed an out-of-the-way booth near the back of the diner.

"Tell me what happened." Leah slid onto the bench seat facing the front of the restaurant, anxious to hear the news.

Carlton sat next to her. Close. Nice. His hand grazed hers and their fingers wove together.

A smile crossed his face. "I hope you don't mind." He lifted their clasped hands.

She shook her head and tightened her grasp as a tingle danced up her arm. "I would like to hear Mark's report." Warmth flooded her chest when she looked into his eyes.

Carlton smiled as he took a sip of his strawberry milkshake. "One of our two suspects was arrested by Mark and his fellow officers on the stakeout at Trotter's. The other suspect stayed in the car after he dropped his man off to do some snooping in the barn. The car driver disappeared into traffic when the police came out of hiding."

"I'm glad they fell for the ruse and don't know where Sylvester is located." She released the pent-up breath she'd been holding.

"I am too." He dropped her hand when the server brought steaming plates of food to their table.

"Would you like ketchup?" The waitress lifted a bottle from her tray and held it above their table.

"Yes, please." Leah accepted the bottle and squeezed out a puddle near her fries. Her first bite was amazing. "Mmm. I usually have cold or re-warmed fries. These are delicious."

"They're the best when hot. The Dudleys made sure all of us boys experienced fast food jobs. One of the things I learned early on was to eat the fries first, while they are hot and fresh." He jabbed two of his fries into her ketchup puddle.

"Hey, get your own dip."

"It's more fun to share, but if you insist." He lifted the bottle, and a splat sputtered out onto his plate, making them both laugh.

Gooey melted cheese and bacon-topped burgers disappeared from their plates as they sated their appetites. Leah lifted her icing-striped turnover to her lips and savored a bite. Carlton's cell phone interrupted her satisfied hum inspired by the cinnamon spiced treat.

Carlton finished his last bite of turnover before wiping fingers and answering his phone. Leah leaned closer to see who was calling. She spotted Kent's name on the caller ID before Carlton lifted it to his ear.

"Hey, Kent." Pause. "Yeah, we can manage that. Tamera won't mind. We'll see you tomorrow."

"What did he tell you?" Leah placed what was left of her dessert on a napkin. Worry churned her full stomach.

"Kent suggested we stay at Tamera's tonight. Someone set off the alarm at headquarters. He's got to go check on it and doesn't know how late he'll be. You'll be safer with Tamera and me."

But, how much safer? Leah pushed her plate away and followed Carlton to their vehicles.

Chapter Nineteen

Carlton woke from a deep sleep to the smell of coffee and bacon. The sound of feminine laughter made his eyes widen as he lifted his arms for an overhead stretch. No light peeped through the edge of the window blinds in the room he always claimed whenever visiting Tamera. He rolled over enough to read the illuminated clock on the stand beside the bed. Five in the morning was earlier than he'd planned on rising.

However, last night's exhaustion resulted in a deep, satisfying rest, regardless of the early morning wakeup call via the aroma tickling his sense of smell. His mind and body were ready for a new day, even though he'd hoped for a longer sleep. Thoughts of holding hands with Leah brought a smile that choked away any remaining yawns as he made his way to the kitchen.

"Good morning, sleepyhead." His sister snapped a towel in his direction before wrapping it around the handle of an iron skillet full of half-cooked scrambled eggs.

"Don't you think it's a little early to be waking people up?" Carlton dropped into the nearest chair and started giving his leg the morning stretches recommended by his physical therapist.

"Not if you have mules that need your attention." Leah had a hand on her hip as she pushed down the lever of the loaded toaster.

"What?" Carlton stopped kneading cranky muscles and looked at the determined woman.

"My mules are just across the property line from here." Her short statement seemed to beg for him to understand any implications.

"So? You have people there who promised to take care of the place when we left yesterday."

"I don't like putting all the work on Paul and Josephine's elderly shoulders. They help when I'm away and some weekends, but Shannon and I do most of the mule chores requiring strength. The plan after completing the tour was for me to be back on duty today. With Shannon in the hospital, I worry about Paul's heart when it comes to doing things like mucking out the stalls. A wrong step from an ornery mule might break one of Josephine's bones."

He laughed. "So, you admit they can be ornery. How about stubborn like their owner?"

"Or their owner's bodyguard..." Tamera snickered as she moved steaming scrambled eggs from the skillet to a serving dish.

Leah pulled the browned bread from the toaster and placed it on a platter half-filled with bacon that he'd seen her pull from warming in the oven. "Eat up. You're going to need a hearty breakfast for our ride to my ranch."

"Why not just take my SUV or the truck?" Carlton frowned. He was starting to stiffen from the recent time in the saddle.

Tamera placed a hand on the back of his chair as she set a mug of coffee within his reach. Carlton took a sip of the coffee. She knew he'd need the jolt of caffeine to get his day started.

Instead of stepping away, his sister hovered nearby. "The last time I checked, my horses didn't have any trackers attached. Leah and I already had this discussion while you were sawing logs." Tamera sat and stretched out her hands, not giving him a chance for a rebuttal. He knew the drill. She always prayed before a meal. Taking Tamera's hand in his didn't give him the same warmth as cupping his other hand around Leah's. They both shared a smile before bowing their heads.

Tamera chuckled before starting her prayer. "Dear Lord, please bless my stubborn brother and our friend as they do what needs to be done. Help them to see Your will in their future. We give thanks for this meal and for every blessing You've sent us, especially as we grow in friendship with Leah. Watch over her and keep her safe from those who seek to bring harm. Hold us in the palm of Your hand and give us strength to do what You would want us to do. In Jesus' name, Amen."

For the first time, in a long time, Carlton acknowledged his sister's prayer with a heartfelt, "Amen." He added his own silent plea for Leah's safety and the possibility of having more than friendship or a bodyguard job relationship. The joy of having God on his side awoke something positive in his thoughts.

He gave Leah's hand a squeeze before releasing it to fill his plate. "How about a compromise? We'll take Tamera's horses in the trailer up the boundary road again and then ride in from the cover of the trees like we did yesterday."

She nodded as their gazes connected for a second. "I don't see a problem with taking the rig there since no one followed us when we used it." Leah's cheeks glowed pink, then she looked down to spread jam on her toast. He kept watching as he gnawed on a strip of bacon.

Tamera waved a hand in front of his face. "If you don't use up all your energy working for Leah, I'd be glad to have you do a couple of repairs for me, brother."

"Leah pays better than you," he mumbled while finishing off the bacon.

Tamera swatted his shoulder with the backside of her hand. "Don't forget who provided the food you're gobbling." Her gaze roved between Leah and Carlton. She cupped both her hands under her chin, placing a goofy expression on her face. "It's okay. I see who is more important, and I'm happy to see changes coming."

Carlton could only imagine the color creeping into his cheeks, based on how rosy Leah's face had become. "I'm hoping for a happy ending after we catch the criminals. Once we finish our chores and give time for our city contacts to wake up at a decent hour, we'll make some calls. I'm eager to hear if there's good news concerning the health of Penny and Shannon. I also want an update on Mark's investigation of the crook he caught last night. Kent is probably sleeping in after last night's break-in, so I'll call him last."

"Put Sylvester's vet and Cara on that list of people to call too." Worry wrinkled Leah's brow, making him miss her happy expressions.

"I'm at your service." He wiped his fingers on a napkin and reached for her hand again as he ignored his sister's teasing laughter.

~~~~~

By the time Carlton drove the horse trailer into the cleared area near the gate to Leah's property, pastel-colored clouds reflected the rising sun. They'd taken the time to help Tamera with her and Jim's horses before loading up for their work at Leah's ranch. Carlton identified a whippoorwill's call as he made his way to the back of the trailer. He'd learned to identify bird calls while sitting on Tamera's porch during his recent recovery. He hadn't been noticing the birds lately, but his heart felt lighter this morning and open to their tweeting.

Leah stood waiting behind the trailer. She looked perfect in the morning glow.

"It's a beautiful morning. I'm ready to get back to my mules."

"You've already worked hard helping Tamera with the horses." Carlton had admired the way she jumped in without instruction and provided excellent care for Tamera's horses and a couple of the boarded ones.

"That's true, but her animals aren't my family of mules." A wistful look crossed her face. He fought the urge to give her a comforting hug but decided to focus on her rescues.

"Speaking of mules, when is your next comic strip due?" Carlton had enjoyed watching her put the comic strip together in her hotel room the other day.

Her mouth dropped open as she directed their rides out of the trailer. "Oh boy. I almost forgot about the comic strip. This whole bad
~~~~~

guys thing has been distracting. After we finish chores at my barn, I need to work in my home studio for a bit. During most weekdays, I have a 5 o'clock deadline each afternoon to hand in the strip that publishes a week later. I can work ahead, but I haven't the last two weeks because of the tour." She scrambled up onto the saddle of a gentle mare Tamera had chosen for Leah, named Marcie.

Carlton led his ride to the log mounting block his sister had set up and climbed on the back of Spanky, his favorite gelding from Tamera's horses. The pinto had a good spirit and easily adapted to the difference in how Carlton's wounded leg felt when giving commands with his knee and foot. His sister had several people with leg disabilities who came for therapy and Spanky was their favorite, too.

Carlton's mind wandered as he followed Leah and Marcie down the path to her place. He had discovered he enjoyed working with similarly challenged people. Tamera often joked about hiring him to teach some of her lessons, but he knew she wasn't financially able to take on another instructor yet.

She supported herself and the four horses. The room and board he'd insisted on paying while recovering at her place had gone into her savings account. Most of the money from her boarded horses also went into that account. One day she hoped to expand. When that happened, he might consider teaching part-time with her. In the meantime, he had a job taking care of Leah.

When they reached the edge of the forested land, they didn't dismount like they'd done the day before. Paul waved from the back porch of the house where he was in the process of pulling on boots.

"Hey, you two. You're up bright and early."

Leah returned his wave. "We didn't want you to have all the fun of cleaning out the stalls. Was there any more trouble last night?"

"No trouble, other than tossing around instead of sleeping last night. However, I woke up to a great breakfast. Josephine fixed some of her super cinnamon buns for breakfast. There's a few left if you're hungry."

Carlton rubbed his belly. "We're good for now. Tamera and Leah made bacon, eggs, and toast. If the buns last through until mid-morning, I'd be glad to take a few of them off your hands then."

"They should be there. Josephine cut me off after two and said we needed to get busy doing some chores. She talked about filling the feed buckets after I got the stalls cleaned."

Carlton nodded at the man's willingness to help, but knew Leah would worry about the older man doing all the heavy lifting. "How about we take care of the stalls, and you can help Josephine with the feed?"

"That sounds like a plan. I wasn't looking forward to raking out the overnight mess. After they're fed, do you want me to put them in the field by the house?" Paul walked down the stairs toward the barn.

"Excellent. They can get a little exercise, and we can still see them from the front porch or side rooms." Leah turned her horse to follow, with Carlton on Spanky trailing right behind.

Working together, they cleaned the stalls and turned the mules loose in the nearby pasture. After washing in the mudroom off the back porch, Carlton sat at Leah's dining room table, sipping coffee and eating cinnamon buns.

"These are delicious, Josephine. They're the best I've had in a long time. They remind me of sweet rolls from long ago."

"Where did you have them before?" Josephine asked.

"My mom knew an older woman who cooked a similar bun for the rodeo circuit we followed. It was a treat we shared on a regular basis." He lifted the spice-filled bun in the air and held it close to his nose as the scent brought sweet memories to his thoughts.

Leah put her cup down. "You haven't shared much about your birthmother. What was your life like with her?"

"Mom wasn't perfect, but she loved me and kept me by her side during her travels." Carlton hadn't known any other way of life. He'd had a ball being the sidekick to his somewhat famous mother.

"Did Tamera travel with you?" Leah hadn't missed that he'd not mentioned his sister being with them.

"Tamera is older than me. One time I asked her why Mom hadn't done the same for her. She explained that when her dad and our mom split, the father won custody. Tamera was happy to settle in one place and was young enough that she adapted to her dad's family, when they moved in with his parents. Mom didn't keep in contact. We have no idea why. Once Tamera turned eighteen, she learned about having a brother after she tried to reconnect with Mom. That's when she came to work as a cook for the Dudleys and the boys."

"Speaking of boys, I better put Marty and Sylvester on paper for the next comic." Leah stood.

After wiping crumbs from his lips, Carlton joined her in standing. "I should make a list of calls to catch up on the latest news concerning your threats."

"Could you phone from my in-home studio? I'd love to hear the conversations while I write and draw, if that's allowed." Leah's request was what he'd been hoping for. Being by her side was becoming a welcome habit, one he enjoyed beyond being her bodyguard.

Chapter Twenty

Carlton sat on a stool near Leah's art desk and watched her sketch out a rough draft of two playful mules kicking up their heels. He decided to contact Kent first, hoping his boss would have most of the information collected by now.

"Hey boss, any updates?"

"Yeah. I've got plenty."

"Do you mind if Leah listens to our conversation?" Carlton returned Leah's smile as she beamed up at him. His heart may have taken an extra thump.

"No problem. Most of what I have concerns her case," Kent answered.

"Great. I'll put you on speakerphone." Carlton hit the correct button and set the phone on a stand near Leah.

"That's fine. I talked to my former secretary, Dianne, early this morning. She was able to find out a few details faster than me and use some federal influence to convince people to share information. You mentioned having a gut feeling about Remington Labs out near the farm where the Humane Society found Sylvester. They create vitamin supplements and seem to be a legitimate business turning a fair profit. Nothing raises a red flag about their business other than the man you saw standing near the place. Dianne will keep an eye on them just in case, since she hasn't discovered who really owns the place, other than a corporation."

"That's too bad. I was hoping we'd make a connection there. How about the drone scared away at Bob Walton's farm near Remington Labs?"

"We're still waiting to see if there were fingerprints on any of the fragments and if they match the one suspect we have in custody." The sound of rattling papers came from Kent's end of the connection

"Has he confessed to anything?" Carlton asked.

"No. He called a lawyer who hasn't come yet, so there isn't much the police can do until the attorney shows."

"How about Penny?" Leah added her thoughts as he watched her erase and redraw one of the mule's expressions.

"According to my contact at the hospital, she's still in pretty bad shape. The doctors are keeping her in a coma until she shows improvement."

Leah stopped drawing and shook her head. "I hope she'll recover. She did her job well as an agent when we first started working together. We had a friendly relationship until the last few months. I wanted to give her a chance, but her last words sounded like a betrayal. She did say something about the crooks not paying her the money they owed her for doing something. I wonder if they were paying her off to keep tabs on me or Sylvester. Money was on her mind recently. Do you think she turned against me for the sake of getting cash?"

"I can ask if Dianne can run a check on her financials. Let me write that down. By the way, how was your stay at Tamera's place? Winnie wanted me to make sure you had fun there."

"It was uneventful, unlike your evening. Carlton told me there was trouble at your office."

"It looked like someone tried to get in, but when the alarm blared, they took off. The camera did pick up the image of a dark sedan and a person wearing a ski mask."

"That would be consistent with the car following us the last couple of days." Carlton stood and stretched. The stool wasn't comfortable, and he was beginning to regret lifting manure most of the morning. "Leah wants to check in with Sylvester at the vet's. What is your advice?"

"I suggest caution. We have Cara in place. Call her for an update. If for some reason you do decide to go there, try to use a vehicle you haven't used before."

"Thanks, boss. I agree with you. In the future we need to consider a couple of company cars." Carlton was glad Kent had reinforced not rushing to the vet's.

"Great. I'll let you know if there's any other news when it comes. We'll talk later about buying cars when we are rich and famous. Winnie says come for a late lunch. Maybe I'll have more updates by then." The phone disconnected from Kent's end.

Leah shook her head. "I liked the part about going in a different vehicle. I want to see my mule. I've got nineteen of my herd here, but I want to bring my missing boy home."

"Didn't you hear the part where Kent said call Cara and use caution?" Carlton looked at her as his heart filled with concern.

Leah grinned. "We can call Cara and also use caution when we go to the doctor's."

Carlton shook his head. "What about finishing your comic strip?"

She held up the drawing. "It will take me another half hour to get this inked. My tablet is still in my bag at Winnie and Kent's. I'll need it to do the final touchups. We'll stop by their place for lunch on the way to see Sylvester."

"We need to get Tamera's horses back to her and what about a different vehicle?" Carlton searched for another excuse.

"No problem. Before you woke up this morning, Tamera told me Mondays are her day off from working with clients. We can keep the horses here until tonight. No one will need a lesson today. I do have a car of my own." Leah picked up a marker and turned away from him.

Carlton walked to a window and stared at her herd of mules. They were stubborn creatures and so was their owner. Having lunch at the Russells' home would at least give the older couple a chance to talk some sense into the woman who'd gone from shy to downright bossy.

~~~~~

Leah finished inking the comic and erased a few last smudges from stray pencil strokes. After brushing off any rubber crumbs from her drawing, she closed the pad of paper and placed it in a slim tote. Once she retrieved her tablet from Winnie's, she'd scan the drawing into her electronic device. It wouldn't take long after scanning to do touchups and send the work on its way.

Glad to be in her own home, she scurried off to her private bedroom and bath, to wash off the smell of morning barn chores. She'd appreciated Winnie's willingness to share her lavender-scented soap, but it was nice to use the apple-scented toiletries lining her shower shelf. After bathing, she pulled on a line-dried pair of jeans and plaid top. Opting to let her hair dry on its own, she stopped in the kitchen to grab a pocket full of equine treats.

She headed outside to visit with her mules. All of them except Sylvester were present and accounted for, thanks to Paul, Carlton, and her rounding them up yesterday. She puckered her lips and gave a whistle with two fingers between her teeth. Most of the herd moved to the fence with welcoming brays. Leah gave each one a pat on the nose or an ear scratch as they nibbled their treats from her flat palm. Jenny Lou snorted and bobbed her head as Leah heard footsteps approaching.

"Do you mind if I give Jenny Lou her treat? She earned one after our ride to find the other mules." Carlton gave the female mule a pat on her neck while several of the other mules deserted Leah and crowded closer to him.

Leah pulled a handful of treats from her pocket and offered them to Carlton. "You're going to need more than one treat from the looks of the crowd you're attracting."

"They sure are a noisy bunch." Carlton leaned against the fence and offered treats to two animals at once.

"I've gotten used to their voices. I like to think they are singing."
~~~~~

Their brays both comforted her and met a social need, if one could call speaking with animals a social function. She didn't have many people to talk with other than Shannon, Paul, and Josephine.

Carlton laughed as one of the more aggressive mules brayed as she pushed others away. "Mr. Dudley had a singing voice like that. It was loud and out of tune, but he loved to sing around a campfire with us boys. We joked about his joyful noise."

"I like that idea. I have a choir of joyful singers who are also great to ride. Maybe I'll put that in my next comic or in a graphic novel chapter. Thanks for the idea."

Tamera's horses approached the group at that moment, wanting a treat of their own. They headed for Carlton when he called, nosing their way through the mules. He nodded to the horses. "I still prefer whinnies and snorts, though I did enjoy my first mule ride on Jenny Lou."

"Wasn't a smooth ride like Jenny Lou's worth what you're hearing now?" Leah gave away her last treat to one of the newer mules who hadn't learned to completely trust her. Apparently treats overcame fear. If that was the case, she hoped Winnie had something delicious for lunch.

When Carlton shrugged, she decided to change the subject. "Speaking of whinnies and Winnie, I'm ready to head over to the Russells' place for lunch and then go see Sylvester. Did you get a chance to call Cara?"

He shook his head as he rubbed one of the horse's ears. "No. I decided to wait and see if Kent heard from her when we eat."

Leah cringed. She really needed the reassurance of talking to the doctor about Sylvester. The vet specifically messaged about wanting to share about the object removed from her mule during an operation.

"Let's go get in my car. I'm anxious to find out what Dr. Sanders found."

She stalked off to the shed where her vehicle was located. It was one of the last things she'd accepted from her father.

A farm truck served for most of her travels with or without mules, but she kept the gifted car maintained and used it occasionally. One of Paul's weekend duties was to take it out on a Sunday drive and make sure the gas tank was full. She doubted he'd had time yesterday with all the excitement, but the vehicle was probably still full from last week and ready for use.

She pulled one of the shed doors to the side and heard Carlton's quick intake of breath. Men and cars... Her father thought he'd done something special by giving her a high-end sedan with sporty features and a name brand that spoke of money. Recently, she'd decided if money didn't come in for the rescue ranch, selling the car might be an answer to prayer. She didn't know much about cars or selling one. Based on the way Carlton ran his fingers across the hood's shiny blue surface, she wondered if that was something he might help her with.

Carlton seemed starstruck as he circled the sporty sedan. "Are you sure you want to drive this when there's a chance someone might try to ram it or run us off the road?"

"I don't really care what happens to it, unless you think I could get enough money, by selling it, to run the ranch for a while. The reason I went on the book tour was to replace finances I lost when one of my major supporters backed out."

"It's worth a lot, but I don't know anyone who has that kind of money. My friends drive used cars and even the price for a secondhand vehicle is sky high these days."

"Fine. Then you can drive it and try to keep from putting too many dents on the body. I'm sure you'll find it powerful enough to outrun any crooks that want to chase us down." She held up the keys, which he snatched from her hand.

"Let's hit the road." Carlton climbed behind the leather-covered steering wheel as she took her place in the matching bucket seat. Once they turned onto the highway taking them back to Winnie and Kent's Forest Glen home, they drew plenty of attention from people admiring the car. Not everyone continued past them as Carlton drove close to the speed limit.

One dark sedan caught Leah's eye when she looked in the rearview mirror during the last few minutes. Her heart sank. "I don't like the looks of the car behind us."

She watched Carlton check his mirrors and nod. "I've been watching them too. It's time to see what this car can do."

Chapter Twenty-One

Carlton whipped around the semi in front of them and pushed harder on the gas pedal. He stayed within ten of the speed limit. They didn't need a speeding ticket or to put an officer in danger if the sedan contained the enemy. The dark car had transferred to the left lane to pass the truck. An exit loomed ahead. Without signaling, Carlton headed down the ramp at the last possible second. The truck provided a moving block, preventing the sedan from following. Carlton's shoulders relaxed as he headed north for a couple of miles. From there he'd get on a county route heading east for Forest Glen.

Leah let out a huge breath.

"Are you okay?" He noticed the frustrated expression on her face.

"How do they keep finding us?"

"If they were our followers back there, it could be as simple as watching us leave your ranch. They now know the mule ranch location. They just don't know where Sylvester is. Someone may have been watching to see if anyone left from there. I am seeing a pattern of dark sedans following us. We're looking for someone who has a fleet of similar cars, since at least one was wrecked." Carlton slowed for a stop sign.

"Maybe a business near Bob Walton's farm has cars like that. Did you ever get around to researching them?" Leah twisted to look his way with a hopeful expression.

He looked away to focus on the road and avoid her pleading face. "I haven't had any time to check into them. We've gone from one situation to another since we met. A threatening rock thrown through the front window interrupted my one night alone at home. Last night I slept like an exhausted hound dog until you and Tamera coaxed me out of bed with the smell of my favorite coffee."

"You did your own waking up for that. Tamera would have been happy to help me with the mule chores."

"Protecting you is my job. I couldn't let her take on your safety."

Leah harrumphed. "Finding out who the enemy is might make your job easier. Would you mind if I started doing some research on your phone?"

"Help yourself. I don't need it for the GPS right now. I know how to get to the Russell home on these back roads." He was enjoying pushing the car up to speed on the open roads between stop signs and small crossroad towns surrounded by farm land. The sporty vehicle was a dream to drive.

"Just try not to take the curves too fast when I'm putting information in." She picked up his phone.

"I don't think that will be a problem. This part of Ohio mostly has roads laid out in grids. Other than stopping or slowing we'll be following a straight line until we get close to Forest Glen." He pressed the gas and enjoyed feeling pushed back against the seat as the car accelerated.

"Thanks for the reminder. I should have recalled the grid. Just let me know when you get close to a stop sign." She bent her head over his phone and asked for his password. It was simple and easy to recall. Heat rushed up his neck when she laughed at his elemental password.

Her laughter was infectious, and he joined her. "What can I say? I'm not a complicated man."

"Right..."

Her one-word response said she disagreed with his statement about being uncomplicated. Carlton cleared his throat, ready to move on. "Do you recall going by Remington Labs when we were at Bob Walton's place? Research them first. I thought I saw one of our suspects near their building, but I didn't get a good enough look to make a judgment call." He waited as she tapped on his phone.

She hummed several times as he watched her scrolling. "This is interesting."

"You sound excited. Please share." Carlton waited as she held her finger in the air and emitted a few more interested sounds before she lowered the finger to touch the screen again. He tapped his fingers on the steering wheel. "Hello, Leah. Any good news?"

She looked up from scrolling. "Like Dianne mentioned, the company creates vitamins and supplements for health and bodybuilding. There's a recent post hinting about natural remedies that act better than steroids. Sylvester may have been starving and abused when Bob found him, but he had plenty of energy for escaping and running."

"I can see that, based on how he did me in." Carlton couldn't keep his irritation at bay.

She crossed her arms. "I said I was sorry. Anyway, I thought it might have been your gun that caused the injury to your leg."

"I know. Sorry I reacted. I'm working on having a better attitude. If what you're thinking is true, then what he did was out of his control." Carlton tried to wrap his mind around that thought and find a way to forgive himself and the mule.

"That is why I need to get in contact with my vet." Her hand was poised above the phone.

Carlton ground his teeth. She had a point, but Kent had wanted them to wait because of the vet's visit with a professor. "Call Cara and we'll at least get an update from her. Kent didn't say I couldn't do a friendly call to see how my fellow Guardian enjoyed Sylvester's overnight watch."

Cara answered after three rings. "Hey, Honey. I'm kind of busy right now. The vet and I are talking about that pony you wanted to adopt from Miss Freddie. Bye, Sweetheart." The connection closed abruptly.

Carlton frowned after hearing Cara's sugar-toned voice and strange message. Leah's mouth gaped open as wrinkles marred her brow. Something was rotten in the state of Ohio.

~~~~~

Leah closed her gaping mouth and then opened it. "Are you and Cara a thing?"

"No. Something's wrong. She would never talk to me like that. We need to call Kent and tell him we're heading for your vet's place. Cara and Sylvester need help."

Leah's hands shook as Carlton did a U-turn and sped back toward Dr. Sanders' office. She finally punched the right buttons for the call to go through to Kent.

Carlton didn't wait for Kent to finish his greeting. "Cara is in trouble. I'm driving there now with Leah in her car. Can you come for backup? I don't know anything other than when we called Cara, she shared a strange message and then hung up."

"I'm on my way. I'll tell Winnie you'll have lunch with us another day. Be careful. How far out are you?" The sound of Kent's keys rattling and a car door beeping filtered through the speaker phone connection.

"We left the outskirts of Forest Glen moments ago. We're only a few minutes ahead of you." Carlton didn't seem to mind going way over the speed limit this time. Leah held on to the grab bar above her seat.

"Good. Let's meet at the Charley Burger parking lot to make a plan, rather than busting in and getting innocent people injured. I'll see you there." Kent disconnected the call.

Leah stared at the phone until the screen went dark. Did God answer prayers for mules? She wasn't certain, but knew she could pray for the people at the veterinary clinic. Cara's name came to mind first.

When she heard the woman call Carlton "honey" and "sweetheart," something hot and ugly that she suspected was jealousy flashed through her. Now that she knew the woman was signaling for help, Leah prayed for the Guardians employee to have a cool head and strength to face the
~~~~~

enemy. She also lifted a plea of protection for the doctor, his staff, and any clients who might be in the office. *Please, Lord. Watch over them all.* Time crawled as she repeated her prayer over and over, not knowing what else to say or do.

A siren blared as they pulled into Charley Burger's parking lot.

"Sit tight and let me talk. I was speeding. We can also use their help if I can convince them we need it." Carlton placed his hands on the steering wheel. "Don't make any movements that will make them think you're about to do something."

Leah clamped her mouth closed and laced her fingers together. She wanted to jump out and tell the officer the whole story, but what Carlton suggested made sense.

The deputy looked in the window. "Sir, did you know you were speeding?"

"Yes, sir. I'm willing to accept the speeding ticket, but I need your help with another situation that's going down. Let me get my identification." After the officer nodded, Carlton pulled his wallet out. His credentials with the Guardians Security Group sat opposite his driver's license. "There are people at the Mill Stream Large Animal clinic that may be holding one of the Guardians Security members in a hostage situation. We have no idea how many other animal owners are inside, in addition to our agent. We'd be glad for your help if you could go there with us."

Leah reached out and put her hand over Carlton's as she looked at the lawman. "Kent Russell, the boss at Guardians Security just pulled in over there. He wanted to meet us here to formulate a plan for going into the clinic. We really could use your help." She added a smile, hoping it would sway the deputy. She was getting good at this people interaction thing. At least, she hoped that was the case.

Kent approached with his hand outstretched and shook the officer's hand. "I'm glad you're here. Did Carlton contact you? I'm Kent Russell, the owner of Guardians Security Group."

The officer shook Kent's offered hand. "I'm Deputy Rob Porter. No. Your employee caught my eye by speeding in that car." His gaze roved over Leah's sporty vehicle. "He admitted to breaking the limit, before he explained the situation at the vet's practice."

"Are you willing to help us?" Kent's firm voice reached Leah's ears. She was glad the man was on her side.

"Let me clear it with headquarters." The deputy entered his cruiser. A few minutes later he walked to where Kent stood waiting near Carlton's window. "We're in. Another deputy will meet us near there. I assume you wanted no sirens."

Carlton rolled his window completely down and leaned out. "That would be correct. This whole incident centers on a mule at the clinic. Someone has tried to locate him, and it looks like they have. I don't know if they've taken the mule from the clinic or if they're trying to find a device the doctor surgically removed from the animal. All we know is that one of our operatives is inside and only spoke in coded words before her phone disconnected."

Leah leaned over the console and spoke loud enough to make sure the officer heard her. "Sylvester is my mule now, even though they claim ownership. When I rescued him, he was abused and malnourished. If we capture these guys, make sure to add those charges to ones of threatening me several times."

"Have you filed reports with the law?" The deputy bent over to speak with her through Carlton's window.

"Yes, with several agencies, from the city police to Forest Glen, and with the county where my ranch is located. I also hired Guardians Security to provide Carlton Marsh as my bodyguard. I assume Kent has a case file on me that you can check if the need arises." Her fist closed as she glared at the men. "We're wasting valuable time here. Can't we go to Mill Stream right now and see if Sylvester is still there?"

"You're right, ma'am." The deputy straightened up. "The other officer is heading for a convenience store around the corner from the vet's clinic. I'll meet up with him there and we'll approach on foot. I suggest you wait there too. Allow the official lawmen to do our job. We'll let you know when it's safe to join us."

Impatience crawled through her body like a swarm of angry ants.

Carlton laid a hand over hers. "We have to let them do their job."

She pushed his hand away and crossed her arms as a frustrating sense of helplessness replaced ire.

Chapter Twenty-Two

Carlton could tell Leah wasn't happy. If he wanted to be honest about the whole thing, neither was he. His desire to be part of the action roared in his ears like an unsatisfied lion as he drove to the convenience store and parked. Regardless of his longings, keeping Leah safe was his job. The lawman was right to keep them removed from the potentially dangerous situation. She didn't seem in the mood to talk. The atmosphere inside the vehicle was heavy with tension. He stood and got out to lean against the car.

Her rejection of his attempt to hold her hand stung. He tried to convince himself it didn't matter, but it did. Another woman, who'd vowed to marry him someday, left him before they tied the proverbial knot. His ex-fiancée had snubbed him when he'd shared his news about the reduced chances of him ever being able to have children. The two situations didn't compare. At least that was what he told himself.

His wandering thoughts said otherwise, so he started listing reasons to break the connection. This wasn't a matter of love and marriage. Leah was only a client, of a few days, who needed protection and that was all he should be concerned with. He heard her car door open and slam shut. He turned to see her walking toward the road.

"Wait up, Leah. Where do you think you're going? The police told us to wait here." Carlton leaned into the backseat and retrieved his cane before limping after her.

She kept striding away. "I'm going closer, whether you come or not. I want to be there to see Sylvester for myself. Strangers terrify him."

"I thought they scared you too." Carlton regretted referring to her admitted challenges. He'd given her a low blow and he knew it. The crumbling sidewalk made it difficult to gain on her. Was any hope of them having a relationship eroding like the cement beneath his feet?

Leah stopped. She turned and stared at him with her hands fisted at her sides. "Well, I'm getting over my fears. I'm thinking like a mama bear right now. My cub is missing and I want to go find him." She spun on her heels and marched away.

"You need to stay here. You hired me to keep you safe. As much as I'd like to be in on the take-down, we need to follow Deputy Porter's directive." Carlton's breathing became rapid from trying to catch up to her and worrying that he wouldn't be able to stop her from walking into trouble.

"Then I'm firing you." Her declaration made him stop in his tracks.

"What about Kent?" His brain started working along with his feet as he hurried after her, trying to think of something to make her listen to reason.

She looked over her shoulder as she stumbled in a hole in the walkway. He watched her lift her chin after righting herself.

"I'm firing Kent, too, unless you want to tag along and see what is happening around the corner."

Stubborn, mule-headed woman. Carlton wanted to shout his accusations at her. Instead, he spoke in a calm voice. "Give me a chance to catch up. I'm not quitting or being fired."

"Good." Leah's shoulders relaxed. She stopped and waited for him. The hand at her side reached toward him when he got closer. "Thank you."

"I am at your service, even if you do take stubborn lessons from your mules. Just keep in mind that you may be costing me my job." His heart stuttered as their hands connected.

Hurried footsteps caught up to them. Carlton turned as Kent came closer and spoke to them. "I hope you two know what you're doing since you're in direct violation of the deputy's order."

"We do. I couldn't let Leah go without me." Carlton gave her hand a squeeze as she smiled up at him. Warmth washed over him like a sauna as he watched her cheeks turn rosy.

"I figured as much." Kent's chuckle suggested more than just their venture to the vet's building. "We need to be observers only. I'm worried we will be the ones arrested by the deputy if we don't follow his orders." He pointed to a row of bushes lining the front and side of a neighboring yard to the veterinary office. "This is close enough. We don't want to interfere with the lawmen doing their job."

"Understood." Carlton held tighter to Leah's hand as they slowed their pace. They walked behind the bushes between the neighbor's yard and the vet's drive to observe the deputies who'd arrived at the front door of the clinic. Her hand in his served two purposes. One, the touch revived a hope inside that he'd pushed out of his life after his ex-fiancée dumped him. Two, he had a way to hold her back if she bolted forward at the wrong time.

"It's too quiet." Leah's whisper pointed out something he'd missed. No animal sounds came from the barn out back. Though several cars sat out front, including Cara's, no one answered the locked door the lawmen pounded on. One of the deputies circled toward the back of the building toward the barn, while the other man stayed in front with his weapon drawn.

Carlton felt Leah tense as she attempted to pull out of his grip. "Wait to see what they find." His command sounded harsh in his own ears. She frowned and wrenched out of his hold. She was going to get herself in trouble with the law and the crooks. Heaven help them all.

~~~~~

A chill filled Leah's arms as soon as she shook free of Carlton's hold. She'd been flashing between hot and cold all day as thoughts about her bodyguard warred in her mind. Her emotions changed quicker than the weather on an early spring day, filled with rainbows, wind, rain, sunshine, and even a hint of sleet or snow. Right now, ice water poured through her veins as she stepped away from the man who was tempting her heart to trust again.

She ran in the open for several paces, then ducked into the shadows. Deputy Porter yelled for her to hide as he headed toward the barn. The anger in his voice brooked no arguing. She obeyed. Staying behind the bushes with no one around chilled her even more until someone clamped a hand over her mouth.

She leaned back, hoping it was Carlton or Kent. It wasn't. Someone smelling of day-old sweat and fading cologne dragged her away from the barn. The new guy was tall and his grip was muscular. Another man in a ski mask joined them, placed a gag over her mouth, and then covered her head with a bag. She caught a whiff of onions and cigarette smoke. The masked felon had to be the pharaoh from the comic convention. The man who'd grabbed her was no mummy though. When she struggled, he didn't even flinch. He was more like a mummy's coffin, tight and stiff, as he dragged her away from where he'd captured her.

"The boss should be happy we finally got her and the mule. Grabbing the doctor is a plus." Pharaoh's voice was harsh. "I just hope my partner will keep his mouth shut."

Leah realized Pharaoh was talking about the man in police custody. She didn't like being clamped in the strong fellow's arms but held on to the hope that they were bringing her to Sylvester and Dr. Sanders. She only lessened her struggle a little, not wanting to give away that she would be glad to see Sylvester again. She let her legs relax into the ground, so the man had to drag her.

Leaving her mark by digging her heels into the ground might help the deputies, or Kent and Carlton, look for her. Her captor must have hauled her from the bushes and then to the next street over, but she became disoriented as she struggled. The man tightened his hold, making it harder to breathe. Trying to judge how long it took before they stopped left her thoughts in a tangle.
~~~~~

Her heart sank when they tied her wrists together behind her back and shoved her into a vehicle high enough to be a truck with a second seat in the cab. She could only assume they were hauling a horse van with Sylvester inside. A long, drawn-out bray confirmed the mule's presence. He was not happy. Rapid breathing coming from the other side of the truck's back seat made her wonder if the sounds came from Dr. Sanders. Worry over the vet's health sent a shiver down her spine. He wasn't a young man. Age might amplify any wounds inflicted by their captors. At least she wasn't a lone kidnapping victim this time.

Thinking about kidnapping made her heart beat faster. This was no boyfriend wanting to milk ransom money from her rich father. Though her ex had betrayed her, he'd never threatened her life, only her dad's bank account. These were criminals that wanted Sylvester at any cost. She'd been a helpless young woman in the past. This time she had her mule to fight for. She'd do her best to fend off the bad guys from Sylvester and hoped Carlton and Kent would somehow figure out a way to follow.

Now that they had Sylvester, why did they want her and the doctor? Did they know more than they should? Would the men kill them, or was there some way to escape? Leah wiggled her way into an upright position and started orienting herself enough to recall each turn they took. The changing sensation of heat filtering in through the truck window from the afternoon sun gave her hints about their probable direction of travel. She listened to the voices conversing in the front seat, hoping for more information as the truck rumbled down the road.

The gravelly voice of the onion-eating smoker scratched its way into Leah's ears. "Barnes better not squeal on the operation. The police got him at that other vet's."

"If he does, the boss will have someone take care of him." The deeper voice sounded from the driver's side of the truck. It held a cruel edge.

"It better not be me. I ain't a killer. I'm just hoping to get out of this alive and make a little money while I'm at it." The pharaoh had a weakness. He couldn't stomach killing. She'd use that to her advantage if it came down to saving a life and pray that he didn't change his mind if he was the one who was supposed to kill any of them.

"If you know what's good for you, you'll do what the boss says, even if it means taking another life. You saw what I did to that fancy woman who was thinking she'd get rich by following the boss's orders. She won't be waking up any time soon for trying to back out when she didn't get all the money she wanted. If she does live, it won't be for long. She'll get an unfriendly visit from me, her good old cousin, Earl."

Leah swallowed. So, the smooth talker named Earl had put Penny in the hospital. If he wasn't afraid to admit to the attempted murder, he'd have no qualms about taking care of the veterinarian or her in a similar manner.

"That don't sound smart, Earl. Murder has a long sentence." The smoker's voice whined, reminding Leah of an unhappy donkey they'd once had on the ranch.

"So does kidnapping, Louis." Smooth-talker Earl cackled as the sun hit Leah's left cheek, indicating the truck traveled north.

Leah made a mental note to remember their names. If she got out of this alive, she'd have that much information to share with the law.

Chapter Twenty-Three

Carlton watched as Leah disobeyed his and Porter's demands by disappearing behind the bushes lining the back of the property where they waited. A grove of trees in the backyard of the house lying beyond the bushes should keep her hidden. He wished she'd not chosen to move away from him, but at least she'd obeyed the deputy to the point of moving back into hiding.

He focused on the lawman pounding on the barn door and announcing his presence. "County Sheriff. Come out now, or we're coming in."

Seconds later, the deputy pushed the sliding door open. He tapped on his shoulder radio and stood to one side. It looked like he was waiting for his partner to come around the office and join him before entering the unlocked building. As he observed the two deputies enter the barn, he heard the distant sound of several doors closing and a vehicle driving away. At least the driver of that vehicle wouldn't be in danger if the lawmen opened fire. Carlton wished Leah would have edged closer after disappearing from his sight. He didn't want her in a line of fire.

Several long minutes passed before Deputy Porter stepped out of the barn alone. The lawman dialed and then lifted a phone to his ear. Kent's phone rang from nearby.

Busted.

After Kent answered, Porter turned and stared in their direction. "I thought I told you to stay put." He glared as he pocketed his phone and stomped toward them, shaking his head as he muttered under his breath. "We found the vet's assistant and your operative tied up inside. My partner is interviewing them right now, but it looks like the criminals kidnapped the doctor and mule. We're going to need federal agents because of the kidnapping."

Kent nodded and palmed his phone. "I have them on speed dial. I'll make that contact now and see how fast they can get someone here." He raised his phone to his ear. "Hey, Dianne..."

Cara stumbled from the barn. She rubbed her jaw where her red skin gave evidence of a growing bruise. She tottered across the ground to stand in front of Carlton. "When Dr. Sanders arrived, I went into the office to check in with him. That's when two men came in. They held us at gunpoint. While they were telling us to head to the barn, my phone rang with your call. I told them I had to get it or my husband would come storming in."

"Good choice. Your phony message is what clued me in to come and help," Carlton replied.

"Thanks." Cara rolled her shoulders and twisted at her waist before continuing. "The mule gave them big-time trouble when they tried to move him without help. They must have been watching for me to leave so they could get to Sylvester without interference. We could hear his braying from the office and were about to head to the barn. The two men got to us first. They needed the vet and his assistant to help move the mule."

"What happened to your face?" Anger rose in Carlton's chest as he studied her injury.

"I tried to stop the crooks. I lost the fight. There was a huge man that overpowered me. He didn't fit the physical descriptions of the two men you shared earlier."

"One of them was captured last night. I'm sorry you had to deal with a different ruffian." Carlton's fists tightened at his side.

She smirked as she shook out wrists still bearing rope marks where the captors had bound her. "The big guy may have punched me, but Leah's mule left a few marks on that brute. I don't think they could have captured him alone. After tying up the assistant and me, they left us in the barn and took Dr. Sanders to manage Sylvester."

"How long ago were they here?" Carlton wanted to move out if there was a chance of capturing the crooks.

"No longer than ten minutes before the sheriff's officers came in. Doc wasn't looking so good when they yanked him out of here. When they took him away he was blindfolded and leaning on the smaller man. I hope he wasn't having a heart attack. His breathing was faster than it should have been."

Puzzle pieces fell into place. He'd heard the doors slam and a vehicle pulling away earlier. "We need to check the property behind here. There was a noise earlier that might have been their vehicle. I heard it when the officers were checking the place." He hurried to Deputy Porter and shared his thoughts.

The lawman asked him to wait again, while he took the lead. "Please follow directions this time, Carlton. We don't need the site contaminated."

"I planned on doing the right thing. I didn't plan on Leah running away from my protection." Angst filled Carlton as he looked toward where Leah had last hidden. She should have come out from the bushes or trees the moment the deputies cleared the situation. Maybe she was still mad at him. She'd be even more upset when he let her know that Sylvester was no longer safe.

"Leah, you can come out now. The news isn't good, but you need to hear it."

He waited for only a split second before heading to where he thought she'd hidden. Pushing through the bushes and into the trees, he noticed disturbed ground. Multiple footprints in a small area had turned up the soil. He spotted a path trailing off to where dragging heels between other footprints led out from the property. His heart sank as he called for help.

"Porter, get over here. I think they have Leah Beach, the mule's owner, too."

~~~~~

Leah struggled as her captors dragged her from the truck and across a hard surface area. If her gyrations made it difficult on them, that was fine. She guessed the material under her feet might be blacktop or cement but couldn't be sure with her face still covered. It sounded like Dr. Sanders wasn't far behind her. His breathing still sounded labored but not like it did when she landed in the truck. Hooves clopped behind them as Sylvester brayed and snorted. She could picture him balking and sidestepping as the men tried to convince him to move forward.

The warmth of sunshine on her back cooled as they entered a building that echoed with each step or sound they made. Sylvester didn't like it at all, if his bellowing was any indication. Leah wondered if this place was where the mule had endured whatever abuse had put him in the malnourished condition before the auction house took him in. Anger reared up inside her chest. She heard a man swearing at Sylvester about some pain the mule had inflicted. The sound of hooves clumping around the building indicated the mule might have freed himself from their control.

Throwing an elbow at her own captor resulted in a slap on her face. The hood covering her head lessened his intended harm. Sylvester's brays sounded farther away. At least one of them was able to move around.

"Hit me again like that, missy, and you'll wish you hadn't." Foul-smelling breath penetrated the hood. The pharaoh guy, aka Louis, was still on the loose and too close for comfort. "If you're smart, you'll cooperate. Do you understand?" He jerked her arm, throwing her off balance as he pushed her down on a rickety seat that rocked from side to side.

Leah muttered a threat into the gag, hoping he'd get the message that she couldn't answer, but glad that he didn't understand the real
~~~~~

meaning behind her garbled words.

"What's the matter, mule got your tongue?" He let out a harsh laugh as he lifted the hood enough to rip the gag from her mouth. "Don't even think about screaming. It won't do you any good. You and your vet are going to get our device back from that sorry mule before anyone else finds out about our boss's little experiment."

Instead of screaming or reacting to the man, she spoke to her fellow captive. "Doc, are you okay? You sounded like you were having a heart attack the whole way here."

"I think it might be a panic attack, but I can't be sure." Dr. Sanders paused and Leah heard him inhale. "My breathing seems to be calming down."

Leah took a deep breath of her own. When her boyfriend kidnapped her years ago, she'd panicked. She understood what Dr. Sanders was experiencing, if it wasn't his heart. All she felt right now was indignation and the courage to fight back for her mule and vet. *Thank You, Lord, for helping me to overcome the past. Give me continued strength and wisdom to get out of this situation, taking Doc and Sylvester with me.*

Pharaoh Louis' voice broke into her prayer. "Once my buddy catches that miserable beast, get ready to operate on that mule, Doc. He has a device under his hide that my boss needs back."

"That will be impossible. I've already operated on Sylvester. Didn't you notice his stitches?" Dr. Sanders spoke at the same time a chair creaked from the same direction. Leah took note that they weren't seated too far apart.

"That crazy beast won't let us get close enough to do an inspection. He bolted as soon as we got him out of the trailer and into the building. I guess we don't need to catch him since you removed the implant. So, tell us where the device is at." Anger edged the pharaoh's voice.

"Do you think I want to tell the location when you've kidnapped us?" Doc's voice was growing stronger.

"If you value Miss Shore's life and your own, you'll answer my question." Scents of onion and smoke came closer to their chairs.

Leah heard a thump. The doctor moaned. She wiggled in her chair, pulling against her restraints, and trying to rock closer to the doctor.

She needed to say something to distract the man. "If you kill us, you'll face murder and kidnapping charges. I've already made several people aware of your cruelty to animals and the harassment you've inflicted on me. My bodyguard and I have a good idea of where you've taken us. Once he realizes I'm gone, it won't be long before the law comes looking for us." Leah stopped rocking her chair from side-to-side as she added more prayers for wisdom. She hoped her last words were correct and would give the crooks something to fear.

The man laughed. "How could you know who we are? You haven't seen our faces or how we got here."

"Let me guess. We're at Remington Labs." Leah made a wild stab at the closest possibility they'd researched.

Pharaoh Louis gasped. "How'd you..."

"Shut up." Earl's deep voice echoed in the space that was evidently the large Remington Labs warehouse across from Bob Walton's farm.

Leah laughed. She couldn't help herself. All the pent-up emotions of the last few days, or maybe the last few weeks of touring, burst out in uncontrollable mirth. "I made a good guess, and you just confirmed I was correct. This place is on top of the list for suspects. I'm sure it won't take long for Carlton to come to my rescue."

Sylvester chose that moment to come closer and brush against the back of Leah's head. She giggled and leaned into him before he snorted and trotted away with a ferocious *hee-haw*. "For another guess, I'm thinking one of you just tried to capture my buddy and he got away again. He prefers kindness over abuse."

"You keep laughing. We don't need you or your lousy mule anymore. We just need the doctor to take us to the device. I'm thinking you and your animal are going to have a little accident out in the country somewhere, while we take the doctor away to find the implant. By the time your guy comes looking for you, there won't be any evidence that we were ever here with either of you."

A phone rang. Earl answered.

"You got the kid. Great. I'll have someone call and let you know when we have his cooperation."

Chapter Twenty-Four

Leah's laughter faded. One of the men ripped the hood off her head.

"It won't matter if you see us now. After your accident, you won't be telling anyone about us or our boss. Go round up your mule and get him back in the horse trailer." Earl's voice was low and menacing. His appearance contrasted with his threats. The man wore business attire and a pair of dressy leather boots.

"So, you're going to get rid of me like you did Penny?" Her courage faded, but she held onto hope.

"Sometimes accidents happen." The man sneered at her as he took off his necktie and laid it on a nearby table. "We'll leave the doctor's face covered for now. If he shows us where the implant is, we won't bother him or his precious grandchild Meredith again."

Dr. Sanders gasped. "What does Meredith have to do with this?"

"Our boss has her in custody right now. If you want to see your granddaughter again, you'll take my men to retrieve the device." Earl laid his hands on Sanders' shoulders.

The veterinarian flinched and bowed his head. "I'm sorry, Leah. I can't lose my only grandchild."

"Go ahead and save your granddaughter, doctor. Don't worry about me. I've made my peace with God. If a miracle happens, or not, I'll see you later." *And I might have a few tricks up my sleeve if Sylvester cooperates.* Leah forced the last of her inane laughter away and focused on looking serious. She'd meant what she said. If they killed her, she knew Dr. Sanders was a Christian and they'd both end up in heaven. Hoping heaven could wait, she thought about what she could do in the meantime.

"You're going to need God where you're headed." The big man lifted her into a standing position. "Call your mule over here so we can get him in the trailer. This time he *will* end up at the glue factory."

Leah swallowed hard. She watched Louis pull Dr. Sanders toward the door, leaving her to face the large, low-voiced man who shook her whole body.

"I said get your mule over here." Earl grabbed her cheeks and forced her head to swivel toward him.

"Sylvester only answers to my whistle." She jutted out her chin and glared.

"Then whistle for him to come." A frown creased the man's brow as he pointed at the mule trotting around the opposite side of the building.

"He only comes when I whistle with two fingers in my mouth. You'll have to release my hands." She needed some freedom to enact the plan formulating in her mind.

"I'll give you one hand. The other will be mine. If you pull any funny business, I'll break your arm in half. Do you understand?" Earl's words came out in a voice low enough to match a snarling bear's growl.

She made a big display of gulping. "I understand. I just hope Sylvester will obey. He's pretty sensitive to people's emotions. If he thinks you're angry, he may not come at all."

Earl paused for a moment before he started untying her. She wiggled her fingers as the man loosened the ropes. It took a moment for the circulation to return as a tingling sensation stung its way through her wrists. True to his threat the big man grabbed one of her arms and bent it behind her back.

"Coax that nasty creature over here and grab his leash." He pulled her tighter against him, putting pressure on her arm.

"A mule does not wear a leash. He isn't a dog." Leah bit her lip to keep from crying out in pain or laughing at his ignorance. If all went right, in a minute the man wouldn't know what hit him and then she could laugh. One of Sylvester's quirks that she'd learned was that he loved turning in a tight circle. She'd used his interest to teach him a spinning dancelike movement. Hopefully the mule would...

"Just get him over here." The man's fingers dug into the shoulder of her free arm as he put pressure on the one bent behind her back.

Leah placed two fingers on her lips and whistled for Sylvester. He trotted closer but paused a few feet away to complain with a loud bray and whistling sound of his own. She waved him closer with a beckoning hand. One step at a time, he moved nearer until she was able to wrap an arm around his neck and lean close to his ear.

"Spin."

Sylvester's head jerked, pulling her up and away from the man holding her. As he made his move, she hung onto his neck and was able to partially wrap a leg around Sylvester as he spun with her on the inside arc. His rump and back legs knocked the large man to the ground. As the mule slowed, Leah slid from her precarious position and ran for the door, with Sylvester's lead in her hand. Pushing it open, she ran outside and climbed onto Sylvester's bare back, using the back of the horse trailer as a mounting block. It looked like Louis had taken Doc away in a different vehicle. As she mounted, she noticed a motorcycle secured in the forward section of the large trailer. If it belonged to Earl, he'd have no problem catching them on the road, but maybe not in the middle of rows of corn.

She nudged Sylvester's sides, and they took off for the farm fields across the road. In the distance she could hear the big man's low bellowing as they left Remington Labs in their dust.

She headed for the trail they'd traversed through Bob Walton's fields. It was easy enough to follow the old trails past where Sylvester made his debut and then head for Bob's house. Leah lifted a prayer that the farmer would be home, and Earl wouldn't come searching for her at the farmhouse before they could get a call into the police. She recalled Bob had a gun. Would he be willing to use it in her defense if it became necessary? As a civilian, would it even be legal or safe for the farmer to shoot at the dangerous man who would pursue her?

Slowing Sylvester with a vocal command, she turned him away from the farmer's home. Heading farther from the road would protect innocent lives and maybe deter the man, who would only be able to follow her so far. The leather boots he wore wouldn't help him hike after her unless he rode the motorcycle. Traveling deeper into the tightly planted fields seemed like the best solution. She crossed a small stream and then urged Sylvester across another field of corn, creating more distance from Remington Labs. The far away sound of a motorcycle engine roaring to life spurred her to keep moving and praying.

~~~~~

Carlton's heart pounded as he sped down the road in Leah's sporty vehicle, sandwiched between Porter's cruiser and the other lawman's vehicle. They agreed to give him and Kent a police escort to Bob Walton's farm on the condition that they would stay on the farm, while the lawmen took a ride by the Remington Labs warehouse. The officers couldn't promise a look inside without a warrant, especially since they were doing this on Carlton's hunch. Their line of cars traveled on a road running north of the farm before turning down the south-bound one where the farm and lab were located. Carlton reluctantly pulled to the side when they reached Bob's farm and parked in the driveway.

Bob stomped from the barn, carrying a rifle and leading his saddled horse, Greta.

"Look what the mule dragged in. I was wondering if you'd show up. I heard a bunch of braying a while ago and figured that mule is back to ruin my crops again. Now it sounds like someone on a motorized vehicle is heading across the fields. I can't afford to lose more of my corn."

Carlton looked at Kent. "I know we promised to stay on the farm. If we're helping Bob, we'd still be on his property. What do you think?"
~~~~~

Kent smiled. "I always dreamed of becoming a mounted policeman one day."

"Do you mind if we borrow the other horses and go with you?"

"You could, but it might be quicker to take my ATV since it sounds like my crops are being ruined already. Give me a second to get the keys, then we can go catch some bad guys." Bob tied his horse to the fence and headed toward the house.

Kent patted his chest. "I've got my weapon. Do you have a gun Carlton could borrow? We may need it. Just don't shoot the mule. Our client, Leah would not be happy. She might even be with Sylvester."

Bob nodded. "I saw Carlton demonstrate his shooting skills the other day. I reckon I can trust him with one of my guns." He went into the house while Carlton and Kent sat down in the two front seats of the ATV.

Deputy Rob Porter pulled in and approached the pair. "Where do you two think you're going?"

Carlton shrugged. "We were planning to stay on the Walton farm. That's all you asked. Did you find anything at Remington Labs?"

Porter frowned as he shook his head. "No one was there. It looked like recent visitors had occupied the space. There was an abandoned truck with a horse trailer in the parking lot. The trailer's door and the front entrance to the warehouse stood open. Nothing was inside but a table and a couple of chairs. The mule left some manure on the floor. Other than that, the place was empty except for what looked like a stall in one corner. It didn't look like the mule occupied that small enclosure any time recently."

"Bob Walton heard a mule and a motorized vehicle out in his fields a little bit ago. We were going to investigate. That may be where the people we're both looking for headed."

Porter nodded. "There was evidence of a motorcycle entering the field across the road from the warehouse. My partner stayed at Remington Labs to wait for backup."

While the deputy explained what he'd seen, Bob stopped at the door of his house and leaned back in. Carlton guessed the man had placed the rifle back inside, before approaching the lawman.

"Good afternoon, officer. I'm glad you're here. Name's Bob. Someone is messing around out in my fields, and they need to be stopped. You can join these two on the ATV if you want."

A revving motor and honking horn echoed from a distance, interrupting their conversation. Carlton ground his teeth. They needed to move out.

Officer Porter faced the farmer. "I'm in. We need to move."

"Sure. I was just getting the keys."

"Good. If we get closer to the action, try to stay back and set an example for our private security guys." He turned to glare at Carlton and Kent as he took a seat in the ATV. "Do both of you have a license to carry? This time I might need your help."

After both men nodded, Bob grinned. "I better get Carlton a rifle."

Carlton stayed in the driver's seat. Once Bob handed him the rifle, he recognized the familiar gun as the motorcycle continued to hum in the distance. He could only imagine how the bike was tearing up rows of high corn.

He laid the gun between the seats, started the ATV moving, and prayed. Prayer was becoming easier since talking about his past with Leah. *Heavenly Father, help me forgive. Be with Leah and protect her. Be with our search party and help us to be wise in our dealings with this criminal.*

He paused. Jesus had offered forgiveness to a criminal hanging on the cross during His own crucifixion. Could Carlton be as gracious? He wasn't sure, but he could pray for the man to have a change of heart. He spent the rest of his waiting time praying for Leah, and the guy trying to capture her. His formal prayer changed to a continuous plea for safety and guidance.

The farmer shouted back at them as he rode toward a path near the barn. "I'll take the lead since I have a general idea which field that motorcycle is tearing up. I have a tractor lane between each section that will get us there faster than trying to track them from that lab."

Porter's voice boomed in Carlton's ear as they rounded the barn. "Good enough for now, Bob. When we get close, you need to get off your horse and keep low. We don't need to be a target if he has a gun."

Chapter Twenty-Five

Leah prayed for help as she slid from Sylvester's back. The motorcycle's roar wasn't far behind them. Maybe if she and her mule separated, and went on different paths through the corn, it would buy them time, perhaps providing one of them a chance to survive. She unclipped his lead, which had doubled as reins during their escape, and told him to run free. He shook his head, ran in a small circle, and returned like a dog playing fetch. If one could picture a mule smiling, it would be at that moment, with Sylvester snuggling his head up to her like he was waiting for a reward.

Doc had said without the implant that Sylvester would have a better personality. This wasn't the ideal time for the change to kick in, but she liked his new attitude.

"Okay, buddy. Follow me and see if we can stay away from this guy long enough for someone to rescue us." She decided to stay off the mule's back. If the man shot at her or made Sylvester angry again, at least she wouldn't fall from her ride and complicate any of the injuries Earl inflicted. Traveling bareback had made for an interesting ride as they'd woven through the tall corn.

The motorcycle's motor turned off. The sudden silence seemed deafening as she held her breath and waited. The man swore at his machine.

"That's the last time I let Louis take my bike out for a joy ride and not fill up the tank."

Sylvester chose that moment to let out an angry bray. Leah cringed. It was obvious that the mule and man had some bad history, but having her mule give away where they hid wasn't the answer to prayer she'd hoped for.

Earl's laughter sounded closer as corn husks rustled with his movement.

"Keep braying, you awful creature. I may be on foot but so is your owner. I see her footprints and know she's walking too."

The sound of the man's angry voice made Sylvester bray again and paw the ground as he turned toward the sound. This time when Leah gave the command to run, Sylvester took off like a bolt of lightning, hee-hawing and kicking up his heels as he galloped away. She turned the opposite direction and did her best to slide between rows of corn without brushing their waving stalks. Keeping the late afternoon sun on the left side of her face, she made the Walton farmhouse her goal. Another angry shout sounded, followed by a distant answer from Sylvester.

"Keep making noise, you crazy mule." Earl's voice was not close either.

Good. Her mule was leading the man farther away and keeping his distance as he ran. She tensed as the clomping of hooves and the hum of another motorized vehicle came closer.

"He must have gotten off that motorcycle and took off on foot. At least he won't be tearing up any more of my corn." The sound of Bob Walton's voice offered her hope.

"Yelling every few minutes will make it easier to track his movement. I want Mr. Walton to hang back and let me do my job. You Guardians Security guys can follow and back me up if you are willing to follow my lead. I need you to dismount so he can't spot you coming." Was that Deputy Porter's voice? Leah couldn't believe her ears.

"Carlton?" Leah hurried through the tall growth standing between them and spotted the deputy sitting in an ATV, with Carlton and Kent. Bob was near them on his horse.

Carlton turned her direction. "Leah, you need to head back to the farm with Bob. You'll both be safer there. You can take the ATV."

Bob climbed from his horse and headed toward the vehicle that the other men were vacating.

Another irate shout rang out. Braying answered, but this time it came from a closer location. Sylvester's hooves pounded as he neared where they stood.

Leah cringed. "I'll wait for Sylvester. If my prediction is correct, he is heading back this way to try to find me and that man will be coming after him."

"Will Sylvester let you ride him back to my barn?" Bob asked.

"If I can catch him, but my mule isn't being quiet about this situation. However, he may be the bait to lure Earl close enough for the deputy to capture that evil man."

"You have his name?" Porter turned toward Leah.

"Yeah. His and the pharaoh's first names are Earl and Louis. They have a boss who wants Sylvester's implant back. Louis took Dr. Sanders to retrieve the device from the college science department. I'm worried about Doc's health. He was breathing hard while they held us at the warehouse."

Another shout reverberated through the cornfield and Sylvester replied from close by. Leah whistled. The mule came running to her side as Bob's horse Greta snorted and neighed. In the distance, sirens wailed.

Deputy Porter held out a hand for silence, which did little to make the animals quiet down. "I hear my backup officers." He pushed the button on his shoulder radio. "Deputy Derrick, we found the female kidnap victim and her mule out in the cornfields across from Remington Labs. One perp is trying to find them by shouting to make the mule go into a braying fit. The man, with a first name of Earl, is getting closer to my location. Send a couple of deputies down the tracks left by a motorcycle in the cornfield and come from your direction by the lab. If the suspect runs, be ready."

"On it, sir."

Another shout filled the air from a closer location. Sylvester and Greta let out a barrage of noise. Leah hugged Sylvester's neck and led him near Carlton. "Can you help me get on Sylvester?"

"Porter suggested we stay down low so we aren't targets. Stay here with Bob or head to the farmhouse while I help Porter search for the perp?"

She nodded but didn't plan on staying back. Seeing this through made her courage grow.

Leah listened as the lawman cupped a hand to his mouth and shouted, "This is Deputy Porter. We know you're out there, Earl. I've got officers following your trail and armed men with me. Put down your weapon and surrender."

Cornstalks rustled. Leah guessed that Earl had no plans for surrender since the sound of running feet and moving plants grew fainter as the man hurried away. Relief filled Leah. At least he hadn't used his weapon on the people she knew, and was running away like a coward.

Porter looked at Carlton and Kent. "Are you two ready for a little roundup?"

The men nodded. Feeling left out, Leah made up her mind to help any way she could. Bob looked over in her direction and asked, "Are you ready to ride back home with me?"

She shook her head.

Bob grinned as he sat in the ATV holding Greta's reins. He leaned closer and lowered his voice so only she heard him. "That's what I hoped you'd say. We'll lay back and help."

She nodded and focused on what the lawman was saying.

"If he shoots, you need to back off and let me handle this." Porter walked forward with Carlton and Kent flanking out to each side. Bob and Leah came at a slower pace, scanning the area as they went and trying to keep out of sight.

~~~~~

Carlton pulled abreast of the deputy and signaled with his hands that he'd go right as the lawman went straight ahead. Kent went left as they encircled the movement in the waving tassels.

"We've got you cornered, mister. Give up," the deputy shouted.

A shot rang out. Porter fell to the ground, grabbing his leg. The sound of hoofbeats filled the air. Greta must have escaped.

Porter's agonized voice pierced the air. "I'm hit. Cover for me, guys." His radio beeped as he contacted the other officers. "Derrick, I'm down. Repeat, officer down. Be aware I have a couple of civilians with license to carry with me."

The radio squawked with Derrick's acknowledgement. "We're still too far away to help, but coming as fast as we can. We'll take care around your civilians."

Carlton limped closer. "How bad are you?"

The officer rolled to a seated position. "The bullet grazed me. I should survive." He scooted into a row of corn with his hand pressed to his thigh. "I'm going to lay low for a bit and be your eyes and ears. Keep trying to herd him this way or toward the deputies coming from the lab. If he comes at me, I'll shoot. You two need to avoid using your guns."

"Got it." Carlton took note of where Porter sat in relation to a tree in the middle of the field. Then he limped toward the last spot where they'd seen movement. Kent did the same, but took a parallel path.

Carlton didn't have to wait long before a burly man plowed toward him on the back of Greta. If it hadn't been a dangerous situation, he would have laughed at the sight full of contrast.

The whites of the horse's eyes signaled the mare's distress. Carlton couldn't tell who was in control, the rider or the horse. The man clung to the saddle horn while yelling for the horse to go faster. One of his boots wasn't in a stirrup as he bounced along and with each bounce it kicked the mare's side. She was breathing hard from the weight she carried and started slowing after she passed the two Guardians operatives.

Carlton started to approach with caution, when a rope curled through the air and lassoed the big man named Earl. The line stretched tight with Bob holding the other end of the rope. The guy fell over the mare's rump and landed with a thud. His gun bounced away safely as the man was dragged backwards by Bob tugging on the rope. Leah leapt into view. Faster than he'd ever seen anyone move, she started hog-tying the man's hands with the lead she'd been using to guide Sylvester. When Bob released his lasso, she continued by tying Earl's feet together with the rest of the rope. By the time she was through, Carlton doubted the man could even fidget.
~~~~~

Carlton burst out laughing. "I think you might have a hidden talent as the fastest bulldogging woman I've ever seen."

She grinned and pumped her fists in triumph. "We got one man. Now we need to rescue Dr. Sanders."

"Do you have any idea where to start?" Kent asked.

"They were making him take them to the implant. When Carlton and I called Cara on Sunday, she said the doctor planned to give it to a chemistry professor at the college. I don't know what professor or where to find him, other than somewhere on campus."

Kent approached as they discussed how to find the professor. "My foster granddaughter was adopted by a professor at the college. I'll call him and see if he has access to a list of instructors in the chemistry department."

While they waited for Kent to get the information about the professor, the other deputies arrived on foot. Derrick took charge. He contacted an ambulance driver to head for the Walton farmhouse. From there, Bob would lead them down his tractor lane to transport Porter to the hospital. By the time Carlton led Derrick to Porter's location, the deputy's face had grown pale, and he'd weakened, despite his claim that he only had a flesh wound. The blood staining his clothing indicated there might be something more serious.

Carlton returned to where Leah stood near the bound man, shaking a finger in his face. She threw question after question his way. He refused to answer and glared as she continued her barrage.

"What is in that device? Why were you experimenting on a mule? Why did you try to run away from the law?" She lifted her hands and shook her head before giving up.

Carlton heard Kent chuckle as he approached. "I don't think he's going to share anything. We'll let the federal agents deal with him when the sheriff's office finishes their questioning. I called Professor Scott Hallmark and my former secretary Dianne. Scott said the chemistry department is small and there are only two full-time professors. He gave me their names and shared the name of the building their neighboring offices are in. Dianne's new boss will meet Carlton and me at the campus with a team, providing a federal presence because of the kidnapping charges that our felons will incur."

Leah crossed her arms. "I'm coming too. I want to see this thing through to the end."

Carlton looked at Kent. "I'll try to keep her safe outside while the agents take down our criminal."

Chapter Twenty-Six

When Kent asked to drive Leah's car to the college campus, she agreed. Everyone wanted a chance at the toy her father had given her. The sport sedan's engine purred as they traveled to their destination. The men's conversation moved to horsepower and acceleration as her thoughts turned inward.

Had her father's gift of the car been an attempt to buy her love? Did that mean he did love her? His renown had made her want to stay away from his coattails. Now her fame was causing enough troubles of its own. It stung that Penny had betrayed her over money to supposedly help her parents.

Shannon and Penny were both in the hospital, suffering because of Sylvester's implant. Doc and his granddaughter were both in danger. Had Leah's fame or ability to make money brought them all to this point? Had it been worth it to distance herself from her father, only to end up in a similar situation without him in her life?

Help me, Lord. I need my family and friends back in my life. Forgive me for pushing my father away. Our relationship wasn't always close, but he must have cared in his own way. Be with Penny and Shannon in the hospital. Watch over their medical teams. Keep Doc, his granddaughter, and the chemistry professor safe from harm. Too many people have been hurt. Open the door to a renewed relationship with my father. It has been too long. If it's possible, may he welcome this prodigal home. She continued to pray during the rest of the drive to the college campus.

Kent pulled the car into a parking space next to three dark SUV's and a couple of police cruisers. "You've got a nice car, Leah."

"Thanks. It was a gift from my father. I should drive it more often."

Carlton swiveled in the front seat and looked at her with raised eyebrows.

"I'm thinking that I may be the one who needs to bridge the gap that I opened in my family." She shrugged at his questioning look. "Shouldn't we be running into the building to rescue Doc?" She squirmed in the back seat of the two-door vehicle, not having a way to extract herself from the car until the men got out.

"This time we are waiting. It looks like the federal agents are already inside. Local police have the perimeter surrounded. They'll keep us informed." Kent's voice was firm.

Leah huffed before she leaned back to wait. She couldn't believe she'd become so bold in the space of a few days. Having Carlton and Kent watching over her had awakened strength she'd forgotten she had as a headstrong child. She needed people. She needed family. The realization slapped her across the face. Things needed to change.

A rap on the window broke into her reverie. A uniformed woman stood outside the window wearing a protective vest. A K-9 dog stood at her side.

Kent rolled the window down. "Hey, Officer Miller. What did you find?"

Leah recognized the K-9 officer from the rescue team when they found Penny at the fence. She leaned closer to hear what the policewoman was sharing.

"The professor, veterinarian, and granddaughter were tied up in the chemistry office. The perps got the device, but not before the professor analyzed both the implant and a blood sample from the mule. The implant was slowly releasing an undetectable super steroid into the animal's system, perfect for an animal or human to win a race without showing steroid use. The professor didn't make the crooks aware that he had the test results stored in his computer. If we catch these guys, we'll have the evidence. He still has the blood sample. All the kidnap victims are now safe."

Not everyone was safe. Leah gasped. "We need to go to the hospital. Earl admitted to me earlier that he was the one who put Penny in the condition she is in and threatened to take care of her if she woke up. He's in custody now, but what if their boss tells Louis to make sure she doesn't recover?"

Kent started dialing his phone at the same time as the K-9 officer. Leah heard the woman talking to the hospital in the background when Kent's doctor friend answered. He put the phone on speaker and pulled out of the parking place. He sped toward the hospital.

"Artie, Penny Barrington is in danger. You need to put security on her ASAP."

"I was just about to call. I thought you said she didn't have family other than some elderly parents. There was a platinum blonde woman in her room a few minutes ago who claimed she was Penny's sister."

"Get her out of there and make sure nothing has changed in Penny's status."

"The woman already left. Here comes security now. You must have let them know."

"A K-9 officer just called the hospital. I'm glad for the quick response. We're pulling in the parking lot right now. Get Penny checked, stat. Who knows what that woman did to your patient?"

Kent slammed on the brakes and jumped from the car. Leah pulled herself from the back seat on the driver's side. Carlton joined them as they rushed for the sliding doors, nearly colliding with a platinum blonde. The distinctive hair rang a bell in Leah's mind.

She turned and yelled, "Stop."

It was the woman who had whispered something in Penny's ear at Shirley's Sirloin Bistro.

High heels clicked as the woman ran toward a dark sedan waiting at the curb. Carlton's cane flew past Leah's ear and tangled with the runner's legs and stilettos. When the blonde attempted to stand, Leah grabbed one of the woman's arms while Carlton grabbed the other.

Kent moved to stand in front of the sedan and pointed his gun at the male driver. Federal agents arrived on the scene along with the police. The agents took the female suspect into custody. Leah caught a whiff of onions and cigarette smoke as they dragged the driver past her to one of their vehicles.

The man turned to the blonde. "Looks like they got us, boss."

The woman's lips curled as she spat, "Shut up, Louis."

~~~~~

Carlton picked up his cane and took Leah's elbow as the agents took over arresting the criminals. "Let's go check on Penny's status." He looked at Kent. "Do you want to join us?"

"Tell Artie I'll be there in a bit. I'm enjoying watching my former agents at work." He waved them on as the hospital's double doors swished open.

Leah accepted Carlton's arm. "I hope that is the last we hear from that group of crooks."

"They'll be looking at a murder rap if Penny doesn't make it." He knew from his former life in law enforcement that the kidnapping charges would keep them out of circulation for a long time.

Leah's hand slid down his forearm to lace her fingers through his. "I know she betrayed me, but I hope she lives and straightens out her life. I'm willing to forgive her, though I am through having her as an agent."

"You've set a good example when it comes to forgiveness. I'm planning on going to the country church with Tamera, but I believe I can forgive my ex-fiancée, especially in light of things that are changing in my heart." He lifted their entwined fingers and kissed the back of Leah's hand. She leaned in closer as his heart started pounding.

"Hey, you two. They're taking the criminals away. Let's go check with Artie to see what's going on with Penny." Kent brought Carlton's
~~~~~

focus back to the case as they rode the elevator to Penny's floor. Leah's hand in his gave him hope as they exited and headed to Penny's room where a doctor and a security guard stood outside her door.

"Hey, Artie. How's the patient?" Kent shook his friend's hand.

"She's doing better than we expected. I spotted a pinprick sized leak in her IV bag and stopped the infusion before she took on too much of anything that might have compromised her health. Whatever they gave Penny must have stimulated her. She is awake and asking about Leah."

"Save the bag and test it for steroids. I don't think you'll find any in Penny's blood. The people who were after her did experiments with super steroids that leave no evidence in a person's system." Kent rubbed his hands together and then gave Dr. Artie a pat on the back. "Thank you so much for your quick response. If that woman placed an overdose level of steroids in the bag, I'm sure your patient would not have survived."

"We'll keep watch on her as she comes off the drug. Thanks for the heads up." The doctor led them into Penny's room, where a nurse was busy setting up a new bag of solution.

Penny reached toward Leah. "I'm so sorry for everything that happened. I met Regina Remington at the casino after losing big time on a series of bets. Somehow she knew I was a literary agent and that I represented you. Regina found out I had a gambling problem and said she'd fix things if I helped her. She wanted to know more about your new mule and where you kept him. When I did what she said, she didn't pay up. Instead, one of her muscle men tried to kill me."

"I thought you were trying to help your elderly parents." Leah stared at Penny.

The agent slouched into her bed. "My not-so-elderly parents are doing fine. I feel terrible about the lies I told you. The last time I checked, they'd parked their camper at Yellowstone. They've been traveling since they retired a year ago." Tears poured down Penny's cheeks as her heart monitor beeped from the rapid rise in pulse.

The doctor moved to inspect the machines. "I think that was a good confession. My patient needs to rest for now."

Carlton laid a hand on Penny's wrist. "Would it be okay if I prayed?" His gaze swiveled between Penny and the doctor. They both nodded.

"Dear Lord, please watch over Penny and Dr. Artie as she recovers. Restore her health. We've heard her confess to wrongs and we pray for her forgiveness. Give her strength to face an uncertain future. Help her to look to You for answers. In Jesus' name, Amen."

A chorus of "amens" and a soft "woof" echoed from everyone in the room.

K-9 Officer Marta Miller had joined them along with her dog. "I'll be finishing out my shift by keeping watch at the door. Other police officers will take shifts until the hospital releases the patient."

Leah leaned closer and gave Penny a pat on her shoulder. "Get well."

Carlton noticed Leah offered no promise of any relationship between the two women in the future.

Leah turned away and grabbed Carlton's hand as they left the room and walked down the hall. "Let's go."

"I'm with you. I'm glad this thing is over."

"I'm going to miss you." Leah sighed as they entered a waiting elevator.

"Not if you agree to go on a date with me." He pulled her nearer after the doors closed and brushed her lips with his.

She held him tight and leaned back with her mouth quirked to one side. "I will, if our first date involves taking a couple of my mules on a trail ride."

When he nodded, her lips met his again with a kiss full of promises of a life to come.

The kiss ended when the elevator doors swished open. Carlton smiled as he looked at his future and linked his arm with hers as they exited the hospital. "I'll even ride Sylvester if he promises to go easy on me."

"All I can promise is that life will be interesting." They shared one more kiss before taking their seats in her sporty car and riding off into the sunset.

Epilogue

Leah smiled as she climbed from her car and watched eight-year-old twins Lisa and Libby riding their mules around the paddock. Carlton instructed them from outside the fence, giving them encouraging suggestions. He made a good father for the adopted girls. She'd discovered he had a talent for working with children and encouraged him to pursue a career in education. Kent had shared how well Carlton interacted with his and Winnie's grandchildren. As a former teacher, Winnie had joined in by suggesting he consider working with young ones.

At Leah's suggestion, Carlton was taking online classes, and an occasional night one to eventually enter the teaching field. Until then, he was installing security systems on a part-time basis for Kent's Guardians and helping her run their non-profit for the mule rescue ranch.

Every Saturday morning, he conducted riding lessons for youngsters at his sister's ranch, on either Tamera's horses or Leah's mules. He'd told Kent, "No more body guarding, unless it's for my wife." Most evenings, his focus was on their family and the love they shared. Carlton had also taken over teaching the Sunday school class at the country church they attended with Tamera.

A year after their wedding, they'd assumed that the doctor's prediction of Carlton not being able to father a child was correct. They decided to adopt, which had been their plan from the beginning of their marriage. She and Carlton started the process by fostering the twins for six months and now the girls were officially their children. She could hardly believe they'd been married for almost two blissful years. Now they were a family of four, thanks to their willingness to take on the older children.

Their family wasn't quite complete. Carlton and the girls were going to be in for a huge surprise in a few minutes. His doctor was wrong. They'd beaten the odds. Leah placed a hand over her belly as she leaned against the fence next to her husband.

"How was the doctor visit? Did he discover why you've been so worn out and nauseated?" He wrapped an arm around her and gave her a warm kiss.

"Mmm. You can kiss me again and that will be the only cure I need." She leaned into his embrace.

"Cure? What's wrong?" Carlton held her at arm's length. Concern laced his words.

"You're going to be a great daddy." She gave him a peck on his cheek.

"I believe the girls already think I am." He paused. "I hope you aren't saying I'll be raising them by myself."

"What I'm trying to say is the twins are going to make wonderful big sisters." She gave him a squeeze and then stepped back to see his mouth hanging open. Leah grinned. "We beat the doctor's odds. In less than eight months we'll be a family of five."

Carlton whooped and pulled her against his chest. The girls' mules brayed and galloped around the paddock.

Leah whistled. The mules slowed and came toward her.

"Thanks for slowing the mules down, Mom." Lisa looked shaken.

"That was fun, Dad. Can we ride fast again?" Libby laughed and gave her mule a pat on the neck.

Carlton shook his head. "Let's keep working on basic riding skills for now. Mom has some good news to share."

"We're going to have a baby." Leah smiled at the twins.

"Are you still going to want us?" Lisa's timid voice held fear.

"You are our daughters and will always be part of our family. You'll get to be big sisters once the baby arrives. I'm going to need plenty of help." Leah watched both girls relax their shoulders and grin.

Libby bounced in the saddle, earning a snort from her mount. "Do you have a baby name yet? I think it should be something that starts with an L since we'll have Lisa, Libby, and our mom, Leah."

"Don't forget Grandpa Leonardo's name starts with an L too," Lisa added.

"What about me? My name starts with a C." Carlton wiggled his eyebrows.

"But..." Lisa pointed her finger at Carlton, as the others turned toward the quieter twin. "Your middle name is Lee. I heard the judge say it when you adopted us. Maybe you need to change your name like we changed our last one to Marsh, when the judge made us a family."

"I'll give it some thought, but you'll be calling me Dad for the rest of your lives, so it won't make much difference what I use." Carlton rubbed the noses of the two mules the girls sat on. His affection for both the girls and the animals sent a thrill through Leah.

"I kind of like thinking of you as Carlton Lee Marsh." Leah gave her husband a one-sided hip bump. Contentment rose in her chest as the girls demonstrated their ability to make the mules stop, walk forward, back up, and circle.

Thanks to finally making peace with her own dad, he'd become part of the twins' and their lives. He'd be overjoyed to learn about the baby. The Leonardo Beach Foundation had replaced the benefactor she lost several years ago, and now helped support the rescue mules on a permanent basis.

She still wrote and drew the comic strip, but after the publication of the second graphic novel, she decided to concentrate on her family and the real-life mules she cared for. Maybe, with a new baby coming into their lives, she'd give Winnie some competition and create a picture book about mules.

The End

Discussion Guide for *Hidden Talent* by Bettie Boswell

Welcome to this discussion guide for *Hidden Talent*, Bettie Boswell's fun and faith-filled romantic suspense! Whether you're in a book club, chatting with friends, or reflecting solo, this guide is designed to spark lively conversations about the book's twists, heartfelt moments, and themes of forgiveness, protection, and second chances. We've grouped the chapters into logical sections to keep things flowing—feel free to adjust based on your group's pace. Dive in with questions that mix plot surprises, character insights, personal connections, and a few "what if" hypotheticals to keep it engaging. Grab some snacks (maybe mule-shaped cookies?), and enjoy rediscovering Leah's world of comics, mules, and unexpected romance!

Chapters 1–4: The Comic Convention Chaos and Early Sparks

These opening chapters introduce Leah (aka Mara Shore) and her bodyguard Carlton at a bustling comic convention, blending suspense with budding attraction and hints of deeper backstories.

1. Leah's fear of crowds and her love for mules come through right away—how does her personality shine (or hide) in the convention scene? Do you relate to her discomfort in social settings?
2. Carlton's limp and resentment toward mules add tension from the start. What do you think of his initial skepticism about Leah's threats? Does it make him more relatable or frustrating?
3. The pharaoh and mummy attackers create instant suspense—were you surprised by the quick escalation, or did it feel like a classic suspense setup? How does the comic convention setting amp up the fun chaos?

4. Leah's use of a pen name to escape her famous father's shadow is a key reveal. What does this say about family expectations, and how might it tie into her mule rescue passion?
5. Imagine you're Leah's agent, Penny—would you push her as hard for the book tour, or would you respect her reclusive side more? Why?
6. The moment Carlton uses his cane as a weapon is a highlight—what did it tell you about his character and skills, despite his injury?

Chapters 5–8: Chases, Revelations, and Ranch Secrets

Here, the action ramps up with chases and discoveries, while Carlton and Leah peel back layers of their pasts, including the mule-related injury.

1. The truck stop scene with the tracker discovery is tense—how did it build suspense, and what does it reveal about the villains' persistence?
2. Carlton's backstory with the boys' ranch and his injury adds depth. Do you think his resentment toward mules feels justified, or is it time for him to move on? Share a time when holding a grudge held you back.
3. Leah's conversation with Shannon about the ranch feels like a brief calm before the storm—what does it show about her "family" of ranch hands and mules?
4. The drone chase in the cornfield is a standout action sequence—did it remind you of any other books or movies? How does it highlight Carlton's protective side?
5. When Leah confronts Carlton about his attitude toward mules, it's a turning point. What do you make of their growing chemistry amid the danger?
6. Penny's pushiness starts to feel suspicious—do you trust her motives, or is she hiding something? How does her role as agent contrast with Leah's independent spirit?
7. "What if" time: If Leah had canceled the entire tour after the first threat, how might the story have changed for her and Carlton?

Chapters 9–12: Betrayals, Book Signings, and Hidden Tracks

Tensions build with Penny's odd behavior, more chases, and revelations about Leah's past, leading to a dramatic book signing and escape.

1. The book signing with Winnie and Kent feels like a breather—what do you like about their supportive dynamic? How does it contrast with Leah's strained agent relationship?
2. Leah's kidnapping backstory adds emotional weight—how does it shape her trust issues, and do you see parallels with Carlton's own hurts?
3. The rock through Carlton's window is a scary escalation—how does it ramp up the stakes, and what does it say about the villains' reach?
4. Penny's lunch invitation and the stolen SUV create paranoia—were you suspicious of her from the start, or did it catch you off guard?
5. Carlton and Leah's hand-holding and vulnerability during the drive feel romantic—when did you first sense sparks between them?
6. The cabin scene with Penny's overheard conversation is a big reveal—what shocked you most, and how does it change your view of her character?
7. Reflect: Both Leah and Carlton struggle with forgiveness (her ex, his injury)—which character's arc resonates more with you personally?
8. Fun "what if": If the SUV theft had happened earlier in the story, how might it have altered their escape plans?

Chapters 13–16: Ranch Raids, Rescues, and Revelations

The story shifts to high-stakes action at Leah's ranch, with kidnappings, chases, and deepening bonds as secrets unravel.

1. The ranch raid and Shannon's injury hit hard—how does it show the real cost of the threats? What does Leah's reaction say about her leadership?

2. Carlton's internal struggle with his injury peaks here—do you think his growth feels authentic, or rushed?
3. The drone takedown in the field is clever—did it make you cheer for the good guys? How does humor (like the horse's reaction) lighten the suspense?
4. Leah firing Carlton (temporarily!) adds tension to their romance—what do you think of her boldness, and does it make her more likable?
5. Bob Walton's farm visit uncovers clues—how does tying the threats to Remington Labs feel as a plot twist?
6. The church scene explores faith and forgiveness—what did the sermon on the topic mean to you, and how does it mirror the characters' journeys?
7. Personal reflection: Like Leah, have you ever hidden from the world after a betrayal? How did (or could) faith help?
8. "What if" Carlton had taken the nickname "Cowboy" more literally and ridden into the ranch raid like a hero from the start?

Chapters 17–20: Vet Visits, Close Calls, and Confessions

Action intensifies with vet clinic dangers, car chases, and emotional confessions, as the villains close in.
1. The fake vet clinic ruse is a smart twist—how tense was the wait for the villains to show? Did it keep you guessing?
2. Leah and Carlton's deepening talks about forgiveness feel raw— which confession (his injury or her kidnapping) impacted you more?
3. The stolen SUV and Penny's "apology" lunch build suspicion—what clues pointed to her betrayal for you?
4. Sylvester's surgery reveals ties back to the threats—what do you think of the steroid implant plot?
5. Carlton's vulnerability about his ex-fiancée adds layers— does it make him a better hero, or does it humanize the romance?

6. The escape on borrowed horses is thrilling—how does the rural setting enhance the suspense compared to the city scenes?

7. Reflect: The book weaves Christian themes like prayer and redemption—how do they influence the characters' decisions without feeling preachy?

8. Fun "what if": If Penny had been a true ally from the start, how might the story's action have played out differently?

Chapters 21–26 & Epilogue: Climax, Captures, and New Beginnings

The story races to its resolution with rescues, arrests, and a heartfelt epilogue tying up themes of family, faith, and forgiveness.

1. The ATV chase and lasso scene is pure action fun—did it feel satisfying as a climax? What made Bob's role so memorable?

2. Leah's bold escape on Sylvester is empowering—how does it show her growth from reclusive artist to brave protector?

3. The steroid scheme's reveal at the college feels like a payoff—what surprised you most about the villains' motives?

4. Penny's confession and recovery arc—would you forgive her, or is her betrayal too far gone? How does it tie into the forgiveness theme?

5. Carlton and Leah's romance culminates sweetly—when did you know they'd end up together, and what sealed it for you?

6. The epilogue's family focus (adoption, baby news) wraps things up warmly—what do you love (or wish was different) about the "happily ever after"?

7. Reflect: The book blends suspense, romance, and faith—which element hooked you most?

8. "What if" the story continued: Would you want a sequel following the twins' adventures or more Guardians cases?

Whole-Book Discussion Questions

These broader questions explore *Hidden Talent*'s big ideas, character arcs, and lasting impact—perfect for wrapping up your discussion!

1. Forgiveness is a core theme, from Carlton's mule grudge to Leah's family estrangement—how does the book show it's a process, not instant? Share a real-life "forgiveness win" or struggle.
2. Mules aren't just animals here; they symbolize stubbornness, loyalty, and healing—what's your favorite mule moment, and how do they mirror the human characters?
3. The blend of comic convention glamour and rural ranch life creates fun contrasts—how does the setting enhance the suspense and romance?
4. Leah's journey from hiding behind a pen name to embracing connections feels inspiring—do you see her as a role model for overcoming isolation?
5. Carlton's disability adds realism to his heroism—how does it challenge typical "strong bodyguard" tropes, and what does it say about inner vs. outer strength?
6. Penny's betrayal arc is complex (greed vs. vulnerability)—is she redeemable, and how does her story warn about the dangers of chasing money over relationships?
7. Faith elements like prayer and church scenes ground the suspense—did they feel integrated naturally?
8. The epilogue jumps forward—how does the family focus (adoption, new baby) tie back to themes of second chances and building chosen families?
9. Romantic suspense often has high-stakes chases—what's your favorite action sequence, and how does the romance heighten the tension?
10. "What if" the villains succeeded: How might Leah's life (and comic strip) change without resolving the threats?

11. The book nods to real issues like animal abuse and gambling addiction—did any subplot make you think or want to learn more?
12. Carlton and Leah's banter (mules vs. horses!) is charming—how does humor balance the darker suspense elements?
13. Reflect: If you could "rescue" one thing from the book (like a mule or a relationship), what would it be and why?
14. For Christian readers: How does the book illustrate God's timing in healing (e.g., Leah's boldness, Carlton's forgiveness)?
15. Overall takeaway: What message about trust, protection, or hidden talents stuck with you most—and how might it apply to your life?

ABOUT THE AUTHOR

Bettie Boswell has always loved to read and write. That interest helped her create musicals for both church choirs and school students. After retiring from teaching for thirty-three years, she decided to write and illustrate stories to share with the world. Her writing interests extend from works for children to adults and from fiction to non-fiction. At the time of this writing she has eight children's books. She recently joined Mt. Zion Ridge Press as a children's editor.

Hidden Talent is her sixth novel for Christian adult readers and third Christian romantic suspense in the *Forest Glen Suspense Series*. Her other novels, in the related *On Cue Series*, are contemporary and split-time Christian romances. So far, all the novels have taken place near the fictional town of Forest Glen. There is at least one more in the works that will involve K-9 Officer Marta Miller from this book.

Bettie has written other works for the education market, magazine articles, and contributed to lesson plan collections, devotionals, *Guideposts* true story collections, and short story anthologies. She is a minister's wife, church musician, mother of two grown men, has one daughter-in-law, and is a grandma to three talented grandchildren. She loves the arts and shares her doodles, and photography from her daily walks, on social media.

Thanks and dedication go to the team that helped put this book together: Michelle Levigne and Tamera L. Kraft at Mt. Zion Ridge Press, Critique partner Ann Cavera, ACFW Scribes group 201-Mary Vee, Dave Arp, Kathy McKenzie, and Jen Dodrill. Special thanks to my husband David, who has to wait to use the computer when I'm in the middle of a thought.

Praise the Lord for God's gifts!

THANK YOU!

Thank you for reading this book from Mt. Zion Ridge Press.

If you enjoyed the experience, learned something, gained a new perspective, or made new friends through story, could you do us a favor and write a review on Goodreads or wherever you bought the book?

Thanks! We and our authors appreciate it.

We invite you to visit our website, MtZionRidgePress.com, and explore other titles in fiction and non-fiction. We always have something coming up that's new and off the beaten path.

And please check out our podcast, **Books on the Ridge**, where we chat with our authors and give them a chance to share what was in their hearts while they wrote their book, as well as fun anecdotes and glimpses into their lives and experiences and the writing process. And we always discuss a very important topic: *Tea!*

You can listen to the podcast on our website or find it at most of the usual places where podcasts are available online. Please subscribe so you don't miss a single episode!

Thanks for reading. We hope you come back soon!

9 781968 693107